Edward F. Benson

The Rubicon

Edward F. Benson

The Rubicon

ISBN/EAN: 9783337222512

Printed in Europe, USA, Canada, Australia, Japan

Cover: Foto ©Andreas Hilbeck / pixelio.de

More available books at **www.hansebooks.com**

BY

E. F. BENSON

AUTHOR OF 'DODO'

IN TWO VOLUMES

VOL. I.

Methuen & Co.

36 ESSEX STREET, W.C.

1894

BOOK I

A

THE RUBICON

—o—

CHAPTER I

THE little red-roofed town of Hayes lies in a
furrow of the broad-backed Wiltshire Downs;
it was once an important posting station, and you
may still see there an eighteenth century inn, much
too large for the present requirements of the place,
and telling of the days when, three times a week, the
coach from London used to pull up at its hospitable
door, and wait there half-an-hour while its pas-
sengers dined. The inn is called the Grampound
Arms, and you will find that inside the church many
marble Grampounds recline on their tombs, or raise
hands of prayer, while outside in the churchyard,
weeping cherubs, with reversed torches, record other
pious and later memories of the same family.

But almost opposite the Grampound Arms you

will notice a much newer inn, where commercial
gentlemen make merry, called the Aston Arms, and
on reference to monumental evidence, you would
also find that cherubs are shedding similar pious
tears for a Sir James Aston, Bart., and his wife,
and, thirty years later, for Sir James Aston, first
Lord Hayes, and his wife. But for the Astons, no
marble knights keep watch on Gothic tombs.

The river Kennet, in its green wanderings, has
already passed, before it reaches Hayes, two houses,
one close down by the river, the other rather higher
up and on the opposite bank. The smaller and
older of the two is the residence of Mr Grampound,
the larger and newer of Lord Hayes. These trifling
facts, which almost all the inhabitants of Hayes
could tell you, will sufficiently indicate the mutual
position of the two families in the latter half of the
nineteenth century.

Grampound House was a pretty, ivy-grown old
place, with a lawn stretching southwards almost to
the bank of the river, and shaded by a great cedar
tree, redolent of ancestors and as monumental in its
way as the marble, sleeping figures in the church.
It was useful, however, as well as being ancestral,

and at this moment Mrs Grampound and her brother were having tea under it.

It was a still, hot day at the beginning of August, and through the broad, fan-like branches, stray sun-beams danced and twinkled, making little cores of light on the silver. Down one side of the lawn ran a terrace of grey stone, bordered by a broad gravel walk, and over the terrace pale monthly roses climbed and blossomed. Most of the windows in the house were darkened and eclipsed by Venetian blinds, to keep out the sun which still lingered on the face of it; and Mr Martin, also—Mrs Gram-pound's brother—was in a state of eclipse for the time being, for he wore a broad-brimmed Panama hat, which concealed the upper part of his face, while a large harlequin teacup prevented any detailed examination of his mouth. Mrs Gram-pound sat opposite him in a low, basket chair, and appeared to be thinking. It is a privilege peculiar to owners of very fine, dark grey eyes, to appear to be thinking whenever they are not talking.

Mr Martin finished his tea, and lit a cigarette.

'They've begun cutting the corn,' he said; 'it's very early.'

Mrs Grampound did not answer, and her brother, considering that he had made his sacrifice on the altar of conversation, relapsed into silence again.

Perhaps the obvious inference that the summer had been hot reminded her that the day was also hot, for in a minute or two she said,—

'Dear Eva! what a stifling journey she will have. She comes back to-night; she ought to be here by now.'

'Where has she been staying?'

'At the Brabizons. Lord Hayes was there. He comes home at the end of the week; his mother arrived yesterday.'

'The old witch,' murmured Mr Martin.

'Yes, but very old,' said she, whose mind was apparently performing obligato variations on the theme of the conversation. 'Haven't you noticed—'

She broke off, and presumably continued the obligato variations.

Mr Martin showed no indications of having noticed anything at all, and the faint sounds of the summer evening pursued their whisperings unchecked, until the distant rumble of carriage wheels began to overscore the dim noises, and came to a long pause, after a big crescendo, before the front door.

'That will be Eva,' said her mother, filling up the teapot; 'they will tell her we are here.'

A few minutes afterwards, the drawing-room window was opened from inside, and a girl began to descend the little flying staircase.

Apparently she was in no hurry, for she stooped to stroke a kitten that was investigating the nature of blind cord with an almost fanatical enthusiasm. The kitten was quite as eager to investigate the nature of the human hand, and flew at Eva's outstretched fingers, all teeth and claws.

'You little brute!' she remarked, shaking it off 'Your claws want cutting. Oh! you are rather nice Come, Kitty.'

But the kitten was indignant, and bounced down the stairs in front of her, sat down on the path at the bottom, and pretended to be unaware of her existence. Eva stopped to pluck a rose from a standard tree, and fastened it in her dress. Her foot was noiseless on the soft grass, and neither her uncle nor mother heard her approaching.

'The brute scratched me,' she repeated as she neared them; 'it's claws want cutting.'

Mrs Grampound was a little startled, and got up quickly.

'Oh, Eva, I didn't hear you coming. I was just saying it was time you were here. How are you, and have you had a nice time?'

'Yes, quite nice; but the Brabizons are rather stupid people. Still, I enjoyed myself. I didn't see you, Uncle Tom; anyhow, I can't kiss you with that hat on.'

She touched the top of his Panama hat lightly with the tips of her fingers, and sat down in her mother's chair, who was pouring her out a cup of tea.

'We had a tiresome journey,' she went on. 'Why will people live in Lancashire? Is this your chair, mother?'

Mr Martin got up.

'I'm going in,' he said; 'you can have mine. At least, I'm going for a ride. Is the tea good, Eva?—it has been made for some time—or shall I tell them to send you out some more?'

'It seems to me very bad,' said Eva, sipping it.

'Yes, I should like some more. Are you going for a ride? Perhaps I'll come.'

'Yes, it's cooler now,' said he. 'Do come with me.'

'Will you order my horse, then, if you are going in? Perhaps you'd better tell them to have it ready only, and not to bring it round. I won't come just yet, anyhow. If I'm not ready, start without me, and I daresay I'll follow you, if you tell me where you are going.'

'I want to ride up to the Whitestones' to see him.'

'Very well, I daresay I shall follow you.'

Mr Martin stood looking rather like a servant receiving orders. Eva always managed to make other people assume subordinate positions.

'How long do you think you will be?' he asked.

'Perhaps half-an-hour. But don't wait for me.'

Eva threw off her hat impatiently.

'I have been horribly hot and dusty all day,' she said, 'and there was nearly an accident; at least, there was a bit of an accident. We were standing in a siding for the express to pass, and we weren't far enough back or far enough forward or something, and it crashed through a bit of the last carriage. That is what made me so late. It is very stupid that people, whose only business is to see about trains, can't avoid that sort of thing.'

'My darling Eva,' said her mother, 'were you in the train?'

'Yes; in the next carriage—I and Lord Hayes. He was dreadfully nervous all the rest of the way. That is so silly. It is inconceivable that two accidents should happen on the same day to the same train.'

'I thought he wasn't coming back till the end of the week.'

'Yes, but he changed his mind and came with me,' said Eva. 'The Brabizons were furious. I sha'n't go there again. Really, people are very vulgar. I owe him three-and-sixpence for lunch. He said he would call for it, if he might—he always asks leave—to-morrow morning.'

Mrs Grampound did not reply, but the obligato variations went on jubilantly. Eva was lying back in her chair, looking more bored than ever with this stupid world. Her mother's eyes surveyed the slender figure with much satisfaction. It really was a great thing to have such a daughter. And Lord Hayes had changed the day of his departure obviously in order to travel with Eva, and he was coming to call to-morrow morning in order to ask for three-and-six!

Eva, quite unconscious of this commercial scrutiny, was swinging her hat to and fro, looking dreamily out over the green distances.

'On the whole, I sha'n't go for a ride,' she said at length. 'I think I'll sit here with you, if you've got nothing to do; I rather want to talk to you.'

'Certainly, dear,' said her mother; 'but hadn't you better send word to the stables? Then they needn't get Starlight ready. I must go into the house to get my work, but I sha'n't be a moment. I wonder what you want to talk to me about.'

'No,' said Eva, 'don't get your work. You can't talk when you are working. Besides, I daresay I shall go later. Leave it as it is.'

' Dear Eva,' said Mrs Grampound, ' I am so anxious to hear what you have to say. Shall I be pleased ? '

' I don't know,' said Eva, slowly. 'Well, the fact is that Lord Hayes—well—will have something to say

to me when he comes for the three-and-six. He
would have said it at the Brabizons, only I didn't
allow him, and he would have said it in the train,
only I said I couldn't bear people who talked in the
train. I may be wrong, but I don't think I am. I
like him, you know, very much ; he is not so foolish
as most people. But I do not feel sure about it.'

'My darling Eva,' began her mother with solemn
gladness.

'It's all rather sudden,' Eva interrupted. 'I want
to wait a little first. Do you know, I think I shall
be out to-morrow when he comes, or I might send
him the three-and-six by post. He is not stupid ;
he would easily understand what I meant.'

To say that this was the cherished dream of her
mother's heart would almost be understating the
fact, and now the cherished dream was perhaps going
to be transformed into a most cherishable reality.
Mrs Grampound, if not knowing exactly how to deal
with Eva, at least was conscious of her ignorance
and was cautious.

'Yes, darling, it's very sudden,' she said. 'Don't
do anything in a hurry—of course I know how
heavy the responsibilities will seem to you, as they

must to every young girl who goes out from the what's-its-name of home life, and all that sort of thing, to those very much wider spheres, but you will do your best, dear, I know. Eva, darling, I must kiss you.'

Mrs Grampound surged out of her chair, and bent over Eva to kiss her. Eva received the kiss with absolute passivity, but sorry, perhaps, a moment afterwards, for her want of responsiveness, bent forward and kissed her again.

' It wasn't exactly the responsibilities I was thinking of,' she said ; ' it was '—she got up from her chair quickly, and stood quite still, looking down over the lawn to the reddening sunset—' it was that I am not quite sure about myself.'

Mrs Grampound seized hold of anything tangible which Eva's speech conveyed, and sympathised with it.

' Yes, darling, I know,' she said. ' Just wait a little, and think about it. I think your plan about not seeing him to-morrow is very wise. He will, probably, in any case, write to your father first. It is very faint praise to say that he is not so foolish as most people. A most brilliant and well-informed man! He was telling me, the other day, about a flower he has in his conservatory which ate flies or something of the sort, which seems to me most extraordinary. Such an admirable land-lord, too. He has just built some new labourers' cottages in Hayes, and I declare I want to go and live in them myself. I feel sure he will write to your father, and, no doubt, he will talk to you about it.'

'You would like it, then, would you?' said Eva. 'Tell me exactly what you think?'

Mrs Grampound had a very decided opinion about it, and she expressed herself fully.

'Darling, that is so sweet of you. Ah, how can I have but one opinion! It is a girl's duty to marry as well as she can. This is a brilliant match. I know so many mothers—good, conscientious mothers—who think only of their children's happi-ness, who would give anything to have Lord Hayes as their son-in-law. A mother's happiness lies in the happiness of her children. They are bone of her bone, and all that sort of thing. How can they but wish for and pray for their happiness! You see, Eva, you are quite poor; your father will leave you next to nothing. Riches are a great blessing, because they enable you to do so much good. Of course they are not everything, and if you wanted to marry that dreadful Lord Symonds, whom they tell such horrible stories about, I would fall down on my knees and beseech you not to mind about poverty, or anything else. Or if I thought you would not be happy, for it is your duty to be happy. But this is exceptional in every way. You get position, wealth, title and a good husband. No one can deny that the aristocracy is the best class to marry into; indeed, for you it is the only class, and you bring him nothing but the love he bears you, of course, and your beauty.'

'Yes; he pays a long price for my beauty,' said Eva, meditatively.

'My dear Eva, we are all given certain natural advantages—or, if they are withheld, you may be sure that is only a blessing in disguise—talents, beauty, and so on—and it is our clear duty to make the most of them. Beauty has been given you in a quite unusual degree, and it is your duty to let it find its proper use. Don't you remember the parable of the ten talents? We had

it in church only last Sunday, and I remember
at the time that I was thinking of you and Lord
Hayes, which was quite a remarkable coincidence.
And then the good you can do as Lady Hayes
is infinitely greater than the good you can do
as the wife of a poor man. You have to look
at the practical side of things, too. Ah, dear me,
if life was only love, how simple and delightful
it would all be! This is a work-a-day world,
and we are not sent here just to enjoy ourselves.'

Eva did not seem to be listening very closely.

'Tell me about your own engagement,' she said
at length. 'I don't know what exactly one is
supposed to feel. I have many reasons for wanting to marry Lord Hayes. I like and respect
him very much. I believe he is a very good man ;
he is always agreeable and considerate.'

'That is the best and surest basis for love to
rest on,' broke in her mother, who was charmed
to find Eva so sensible. 'That is just what I
have always said. Love must spring out of these
things, darling, just as the leaves and foliage of a
tree spring out of the solid wood. So many girls
have such foolish, sentimental notions, just as if

they had just come away from a morning per-
formance at the Adelphi. That is not love; it
is just silly, school-girl sentimentality, which silly
school-girls feel for tenor singers, and a silky
moustache, and slim, weak-eyed young men. Real
love is the flower of respect and admiration, and
solid esteem. *Aimer c'est tout comprendre;* and
to do that you must have no illusions—you must
keep the light dry—you must regard a man as
he is, not as you think he is.'

'Yes, I see,' said Eva, slowly; 'I daresay you
are right. I certainly never felt any school-girl
sentimentality for anyone. I think I shall go for
a ride, mother; it is nice to get a breath of fresh
air after a long journey.'

Mrs Grampound rose too, and drew her arm
through Eva's.

'Yes, darling, it will do you good,' she said.
'And you can think about all this quietly. Your
father is out still; he went down to the river just
before you came, to see if he could get a trout or
two. And Percy comes this evening. I will ring
the bell in the drawing-room for your horse to
come round, if you will go and get your habit

B

on.   Give me one more kiss, dear; it is so nice
to have you home again.'

Eva put her horse into a steady canter over the
springy turf, and soon caught her uncle up, who
was ambling quietly along on a grey pony. He
was staying with his brother-in-law for a week or
two, before going back to America, being a citizen
of the United States. He rode for two reasons—
indeed, he never did anything without a reason—
both of which were excellent. Riding was a means
of progressing from one place to another, and it
was a sort of watch-key which wound up the
mechanism of the body. He was rather hypo-
chondriacal, and his doctor advised exercise, so he
obeyed his doctor and rode. He did much more
good than harm in this wicked world, but com-
paratively little of either.

His sister had married Mr Grampound early in
life. She had a considerable fortune left her by
her father, by aid of which, as with a golden spade,
she hoped to bury her American extraction. This
she had succeeded in doing, with very decent
success, but her golden spade had, so to speak,
been broken in the act of interment, for her hus-

band had speculated rather wildly with her money, and had lost it. Mrs Grampound cared very little for this ; her golden spade had done its work. She had married into the English aristocracy, for the Grampounds, though their accounts at banks did not at all correspond to the magnificence of their origin, and though the family estates had been sold to the last possible acre, held, in the estimation of the world, that position which, though it takes only a generation or two of great wealth to raise, requires an infinite number of generations of poverty to demolish.

Eva found the society of her uncle very sooth-ing on this particular afternoon. He very seldom disagreed with anybody, chiefly because he hated argument as a method of conversation, but his assent was not of that distressing order which is more irritating than a divergent view, for he always took the trouble to let it appear that he had de-voted considerable thought to the question at issue, and had arrived at the same conclusions as his interlocutor.

It was nearly eight when they reached home, and the dusk was thickening into night. Mr

Grampound had just got in, when they dismounted at the door, and he greeted Eva in his usual digni- fied and slightly interested manner. The extreme finish of his face suggested that the number of Grampounds who had been turned out of the same mediæval mould, was very considerable.

Eva's father held the door open for her to pass into the inner hall, and Eva, going to the table to take a bedroom candle, noticed that there was a note lying there for him. She turned it over quickly, and saw a coronet and 'Aston House' on the back. She handed it to her father, who took it and said,—

'From Lord Hayes. I thought he had not come home yet.'

Eva was standing on the lowest step of the flight of stairs.

'Yes; he came home with me to-day,' she said.

'Was he with you at the Brabizons?'

'Yes; we travelled together.'

Eva went up to her room, not wishing to see the note opened in her presence. What it would con- tain she knew, or, at least, guessed. Five minutes later, Mr Grampound also came upstairs and tapped at the door of his wife's room. She had not begun to dress, and he came in with the note in his hand. His cold, clean-shaven face showed a good deal of gentlemanly and quiet satisfaction.

'Of course there is only one answer,' he said, when she had finished reading it. 'It is a splendid match for her.'

'Eva spoke to me about it this afternoon,' said his wife.

'Well?'

'She does not want to be hurried. She wants to have time to decide.'

'There is no time like the present,' observed Mr Grampound.

'I hope you won't press her, Charles. You will get nothing by that. She wants to marry, I know; and I said a great many very sensible things to her this afternoon. She wants more than a quiet home-life can give her, and she likes Hayes.'

'I must send some answer to him; and I certainly shall not tell him to keep away.'

'Give her time. Say he may come in a week.

There is no harm in waiting a little. Eva will not be forced into anything against her will.'

' I shall speak to her to-night.'

'Yes, do; but be careful. I must send you away now; it is time to dress. Percy has come.'

Eva, meanwhile, was thinking over the talk she had had with her mother. Mrs Grampound's affectionate consideration for her daughter's feelings, Eva knew quite well, might only be the velvet glove to an iron hand. But she was distinctly conscious that there was a great deal in what her mother had said. She had decided for herself that she was not going to fall in love with anyone; men seemed to her to be very little lovable. At the same time, she knew that, in her heart of hearts, she longed for the possibilities which a great marriage would give her. Perhaps then the world would open out; perhaps it was interesting after all. Her home-life bored her considerably. They were in the country nine months out of the twelve, living in a somewhat sparsely-populated district, and Eva was totally unable to make for herself active or engrossing occupation in the direction of district-visiting or Sunday schools, or those hundred and one ways in which 'nice girls' are supposed to employ themselves. Her vitality was of that still, strong sort which can only be reached through the emotions, and is too indolent or too uninitiative to stir the emotions into creating interests for themselves. The vague imperative *need* of doing something never wound its horn to her. She could not throw herself into the first pursuit that offered, simply because she had to be doing something, and her emotional record was a blank. The pencil and paper were there, for she was two-and-twenty, but she had nothing to write. She was quite unable to transform her diversions into aims, a faculty which accounts completely for the busy lives some women lead.

Dinner was not till half-past eight, and, when Eva came down, the drawing-room was untenanted. The shaded lamp left the room in comparative dimness, but through the windows, which were open to let in the cool, evening air, the last glow of the sunset cast a red light on to the opposite wall. She stood at the window a moment and looked at the river, which lay like a string of crimson pools stretching west; and then, turning away impatiently, walked up and down the room, wondering where everyone was. That peaceful, sleeping landscape outside seemed to her an emblem of the quiet, deadly days that were to come. The slow to-morrow and to-morrow seemed suddenly impossible. The door was open to her—the door leading on all that the world had to offer. Perhaps it was all as uninteresting as this, but it would be something, at any rate, to know that—to be quite certain that life was dull to the core. Then she thought she could rest quiet, and, perhaps, would not mind so much. What vexed and irritated her, was to suspect that the world was interesting and not to find it so, and she was disposed to lay the blame of that on her own particular station in life. Yet—yet—she could hardly say she had an ideal, but there was that shrouded image called love, of which she only saw the dim outline. It would be a pity to smash it up before the coverings came off. It might be worth having, after all.

Her eye caught sight of a book on the table with a white vellum cover. Eva took it up. It was called *The Crown of Womanhood*, and something like a frown gathered on her face.

It was almost a relief when her mother entered

rustling elaborately across the room, and snapping a bracelet on to her comely wrist.

'Ah! Eva, you are before me. Percy has come. I didn't expect him till to-morrow.'

'I'm glad,' said Eva listlessly.

'Such a lovely evening,' continued Mrs Grampound with a strong determination to be particularly neutral, and entirely unconscious of her talk with Eva before dinner. 'Look at those exquisite tints, dear. The blue so tender as to be green,' she quoted with a fine disregard of accuracy.

'Yes, it's beautiful,' said Eva, not turning her head. 'Ah! Percy, it's good to see you.'

Eva got up and walked across to meet the new-comer. Percy was a favourite of hers, from the time he had teased her about her dolls onward.

'How long are you going to stop?' she continued. 'Percy, stop here a long time; I want you.'

'I can't,' he said. 'I'm going off to Scotland on the 12th, to the Davenports. I promised Reggie.'

'Who's Reggie?'

'Reggie? Reggie Davenport. He's a friend of mine. I'm very fond of him. Haven't you ever seen him ? He falls in love about once a fortnight. He's very amusing.'

' He must be rather a fool,' said Eva.

' Oh, but he's a nice fool.   Really, he is very nice. He's so dreadfully young.'

' Well, your not very old, my lord,' said Eva.

' But Reggie is much the youngest person I ever saw.   He'll never grow old.'

' Ah ! well,' said Eva.   ' I expect he's very happy.'

The gong had sounded some minutes, when Mr Martin shuffled in.   He wore a somewhat irregular white tie and grey socks, and was followed almost immediately by Mr Grampound.

Eva had already written a little note to Lord Hayes, and told her maid to enclose a three-and-sixpenny postal order.   She had also expressed a vague hope, so as not to block her avenues, that they would meet again soon.   Her chief desire was to obtain a respite ; the whole thing had been too sudden, and she wished to think it over.   Meantime, it was nice to see Percy again.

' What have you been doing with yourself?' she asked.   ' I notice that whenever young men go away in novels, they always fall in love before they get

back, or get married, or make their fortunes or lose
them. How many of these things have you done?'

'None of them,' said Percy; 'though I've been to
Monte Carlo, I did not play there. It doesn't seem
to me at all amusing.'

'I suppose you haven't got the gambling instinct,'
said Eva; 'that's a great defect. You know none of
the joy of telling your cabman that you will give
him a shilling extra if he catches a train. It's
equivalent to saying, "I bet you a shilling you don't;"
only he doesn't pay if he loses, and you do. But
that's immaterial. The joy lies in the struggle with
time and space.

'Do you mean that you like to keep things in
uncertainty as long as possible,' asked her father,
looking at her.

Their eyes met, and they understood each other.
Eva looked at him a moment, and then dropped
her eyes.

'Yes; I'm sure I do.'

'Even when you have all the data ready, do you
like not deciding?'

'Oh! one never knows if one has all the data;
something fresh may always turn up. For instance—'

' Well ? '

' I was thinking just before dinner that I didn't know what in the world I should do with myself all the autumn, and now you see Percy's arrived. I shall play about with him.'

' I go away in two days,' said Percy.

' Oh! well, I daresay something else will turn up. I am like Mr Micawber.'

' No, not at all,' said Mr Grampound ; ' he was always doing his best to make things turn up.'

Mrs Grampound remarked that things were always turning up when you expected them least, and Percy hoped that his gun would turn up, because no one could remember where it was.

The evening was so warm that Eva and her mother sat outside on the terrace after dinner, waiting for the others to join them. Mr Grampound never sat long over his wine, and in a few minutes the gentlemen followed them. Eva was rather restless, and strolled a little way down the gravel path, and, on turning, found that her father had left the others and was walking towards her.

' Come as far as the bottom of the lawn, Eva,' he said ; ' I should like a little talk with you.'

They went on in silence for some steps, and then her father said,—

'I heard from Lord Hayes to-day. Your mother told me that you could guess what it was about.'

She picked up a tennis-ball that was lying on the edge of the grass.

'How wet it is!' she said. 'Yes, I suppose I know what he wrote about.'

'Your mother and I, naturally, have your happiness very much at heart,' said he, 'and we both agree that this is a very sure and clear chance of happiness for you. It is a great match, Eva.'

Eva as a child had always rather feared her father, and at this moment she found her childish fear rising again in her mind. Tall, silent, rather scornful-looking men may not always command affection, but they usually inspire respect. Her old fear for her father had grown into very strong respect, but she felt now that the convert transformation was very possible.

'You would wish me to marry him?' she asked.

'I wish you to consider it very carefully. I have seen a good deal of the world, so I also wish you to consider what I say to you about it. I have thought about it, and I have arrived at the very definite conclusion I have told you. I shall write to him to-night, and, with your consent, will tell him that he may come and ask you in person in a few days' time. You know my wishes on the subject, and your mother's. Meanwhile, dear Eva, I must congratulate you on the very good fortune which has come in your way.'

He bent from his great height and kissed her.

'I don't wish to force you in any way,' he said, 'and I don't wish you to say anything to me to-night about it. Think it over by yourself. I needn't speak of his position and wealth, because, though, of course, they are advantages, you will rate them at their proper value. But I may tell you that I am a very poor man, and that I know what these things mean.'

'I should not marry him for those reasons,' said Eva.

'There is no need for you to tell me that,' said he. 'But it is right to tell you that I can leave you nothing. In the same way I hope that any foolish notions you may have got about love, from the trash you may have read in novels, will not stand in your way either. I will leave the matter in the hands of your own good sense.'

His words had an unreasonable mastery over Eva, for her father never spoke idly. He was quite aware of the value of speech, but knew that it is enhanced by its rarity. 'No one pays any attention to a jabbering fool,' he had said once to his wife, à *propos* of a somewhat voluble woman who had been staying in the house, and of whose abilities he and his wife entertained very contrary opinions. Eva had seldom heard him express his philosophy of life at such length, and she fully appreciated the weight it was intended to convey.

L ORD HAYES found Eva's note waiting for him when he came down to breakfast next morning, but its contents did not take away his appetite at all. He was quite as willing that she should think it over as her father or mother, and he had no desire to force her to refuse. He was fairly certain that at his time of life, for he was over forty, he was not going to fall in love in the ordinary sense of the word ; that sense, in fact, which Eva had herself confessed she never felt likely to experience. He had had a succession of eligible helpmeets hurled at his head by ambitious mothers for many years, and in sufficient numbers to enable him to draw the conclusion that the majority of eligible helpmeets were very much like one another.

They had ready for him smiles of welcome,

slightly diverting small-talk, pretty faces, and any number of disengaged waltzes; and after having basked in their welcoming smiles, submitted to their small-talk, looked at their pretty faces, and hopped decorously round in their disengaged waltzes, he always finished by stifling a yawn and making his exit. It would convey an entirely wrong impression to describe him as either a misanthrope or a cynic; the charms of marriageable maidenhood simply did not appeal to him. But though he was neither misanthrope nor cynic, a little vein of malevolence ran through his system, and he had more than half made up his mind that he would have none of these. He was quite rich enough to afford a wife who would bring him nothing but unpaid bills; and provided that wife brought him something which he had not yet found, he was willing to pay them all.

That he was going to marry some time had long been a commonplace to him, but the sight of his forty-fifth milestone had lent it a loud insistence which was becoming quite distracting. The thought had begun to haunt him; he saw it in the withered flowers of his orchid house, it stuck in the corners

C

of his coat pockets, his garden syringe gurgled it at him with its expiring efforts to emit the last drop of water; even the toad which he kept in his greenhouse had the knowledge of it lurking in its sickly eye.

He was very seldom at Aston; but in one of his visits there, he had met Eva and had been considerably struck by her. She was introduced to him, and bowed without smiling. He had asked her whether she played lawn-tennis, and she said, without simpering, that she did. He asked her whether she enjoyed the season, and she replied, without affectation, that she had got so tired of it by the middle of June that she had gone down into the country. He remarked that London was the loser, and she reminded him that, therefore, by exactly the same amount, the country was the gainer. Her eyes wandered vaguely over the green distance, and once met his, without shrinking from or replying to his gaze. She was astonishingly beautiful, and appeared quite unconscious of her charms. She looked so radically indifferent to all that was going on round her, that he had said, 'These country parties are rather a bore!' and she replied candidly that she quite agreed with him. In a word, he felt that he might go farther and fare worse, and that he was forty-five years old.

During the next few months, he had come across her not infrequently, both in the country and in London, and at the end of the season they had both met at the Brabizons, where two Miss Brabizons were alternately launched at his hand and heart—*via* brilliant execution on the piano and district-visiting —by their devoted mother, and Eva's calm neutrality was rendered particularly conspicuous by the contrast. His attentions to her grew more and more marked, and Mrs Brabizon metaphorically threw up the sponge when he changed the day of his departure without ceremony, in order to travel with Eva, and declared that she couldn't conceive what he found in that girl.

His mother always breakfasted alone, and spent the morning by herself, usually out of doors. Lord Hayes was vaguely grateful for this arrangement. Mr Martin, as we know, had described her as an old witch, and even to her own son she seemed rather a terrific person. She was tall, very well preserved, and a rigid Puritan. Her hobby—for the most unbending of our race have their hobby—was

Jaeger clothing. She wore large grey boots with
eight holes in them, a drab-coloured dress, and
a head-gear that reminded the observer of a
volunteer forage cap. This hobby she varied by
a spasmodic interest in homœopathy, and she used
to walk about the lanes like a mature Medea, gathering simples from the hedges, which she used to
administer with appalling firmness to the village
people; but, to do her justice, she always experi-
mented with them first *in propriâ personâ*, and declared she felt a great deal better afterwards. For
the practice of medicine-taking generally, she
claimed that it fortified the constitution, and it
must be confessed that her own constitution, at the
age of sixty-five, appeared simply impregnable.

But in the morning her son was conscious of an
agreeable relaxation. He was a neat, timid man,
with a careful little manner, and he inherited from
his mother a certain shrewdness that led him to
grasp the practical issues of things with rapidity.
For instance, on this present occasion, when he
had finished his breakfast, he again read over Eva's
letter, put it carefully away, and was quite content
to wait.

Outside one of the dining-room windows opened a glass-covered passage leading into an orchid house, and he went down this passage with the heels of his patent leather shoes tapping on the tiles, and a large pair of scissors in his hand. Every morning he attended personally to the requirements of this orchid house; he snipped off dead sprays, he industriously blew tobacco smoke on small parasitic animals, and squirted them with soapy water, and this morning, being in a particularly good humour, he went so far as to tickle, with a wisp of hay, the back of the useful toad. That animal received his attentions with silent affability; it closed its eyes, and opened and shut its mouth like an old gentleman awaking from his after-dinner nap.

It was a warm morning, and when he had finished attending to the orchids he strolled round outside the house, back to the front door. The house stood high above the river, and commanded a good view of the green valley; and, in the distance, two miles away, the red-roofed village slanted upwards from the stream towards the downs. He stood looking out over the broad, pleasant fields for some moments, and his eyes wandered across the river to where the red front of Mr Grampound's house, half hidden by the large cedar, stood, as if looking up to his. The flower-beds gleamed like jewels in the sunshine, and he could see two figures strolling quietly down the gravel path towards the river. One of them was a girl, tall, almost as tall as the man who walked by her side, and to whom she was apparently talking. Just as Lord Hayes looked, they stopped suddenly, and he saw her spread out her hands, which had been clasped in front of her, with a quick, dramatic movement. The action struck him as slightly symbolical.

He was roused by the sound of crunched gravel, and, turning round, saw his mother walking towards him. She was in her hygienic dress, and had a small, tin botanical case slung over her shoulders. In her hand she held a pair of eminently useful scissors, the sort of scissors with which Atropos might sever the thread of life. Lord Hayes wore a slightly exotic look by her side.

'The under housemaid has fallen into a refreshing sleep,' she announced, 'and the action of the skin has set in. In fact, she will do very well now. And how are you, dear James, this morning?'

'I am very well,' said he; 'very well indeed, thank you, mother.'

His mother looked at him with interest.

'You've got a touch of liver,' she remarked truculently.'

'No, I think not. I feel very well, thanks.

Lady Hayes snapped her scissors.

'I'm afraid the harvest will be very bad this year,' she said. 'There's been no rain, and no rain means no straw.'

'Yes, the farmers are in a bad way,' said Lord Hayes. 'I shall have to make a reduction again.'

'Well, dear,' said his mother, 'all I can say is that we shall probably be beggars. But porridge is wonderfully sustaining.'

'We've still got a few acres in London,' he remarked. 'Really, in these depressed times, I don't know how a man could live without an acre or two there.'

Old Lady Hayes laughed a hoarse, masculine laugh, and strode off, snapping her scissors again. Half-way across the lawn she stopped.

'The Grampounds are at home, I suppose,' she said. 'I want to see Mrs Grampound some time.'

'Oh, yes; I travelled with Miss Grampound yesterday. She said they were all at home.'

'Ha! She is very handsome. But a modern young woman, I should think.'

'She's not very ancient. She was staying with the Brabizons.'

His mother frowned and continued her walk.

Lord Hayes always felt rather like a naughty child under his mother's eye. He did not at present feel quite equal to telling her what his relations with Eva were. Modernity was the one failing for which she had no sympathy, for it was a characteristic of which she did not possess the most rudimentary traces. To her it meant loss of dignity, Americanisms, contempt for orthodoxy, and general relaxation of all that is worthy in man. She preferred the vices of her own generation to the virtues of newer developments, and almost regretted the gradual extinction of the old three-bottle school, for they were, in her opinion, replaced by men who smoked while they were talking to women, while the corresponding women had given way to women who smoked themselves. For a man to drink port wine in company with other men was better, as being a more solid and respectable failing, than for him to talk to a woman with a cigarette between his lips.

Eva, as Lord Hayes had guessed from his point of vantage by the front door of his house, had strolled out into the garden after breakfast with Percy. She had not told him of Lord Hayes's offer, but she could not help talking to him with it in her mind. It was like a bracket preceded by a minus sign, which affected all that was within the bracket.

'I wish you weren't going away, Percy,' she said. 'When I woke up this morning, I thought with horror of all the slow days that were coming. I don't care a bit for doing all those things which "nice girls" are supposed to do. I have no enthusiasms, and the enthusiasms of the people I see here are unintelligible to me. The sight of a dozen little boys in a Sunday school, with pomatum on their heads, inspires me with slight disgust —so do bedridden old women. I suppose I have no soul. That is quite possible. But, but—'

'Yes, I'm luckier than you,' said Percy; 'I like little quiet things. I like fishing, and reading the paper, and doing nothing.'

'Yes, you're luckier than I am just now,' said Eva, 'but when I do get interested in things, I shall be in a better position than you. I'm sure there are lots of interests in the world, but I don't realise it.'

'Well, I daresay you will discover them sometime,' said Percy, consolingly.

'Who can tell? There are lots of women who do not feel any interest in anything—though, perhaps, fewer women than men. But why does London interest you so? It seems to me just as stupid in its way as this place.'

'I like the sense of there being loads of people about,' said Percy. 'A lot of people together are not at all the same as a number of units.'

'How do you mean?'

'Well, it's just the same as with gunpowder. One grain of powder only spits if you set light to it, but if you were to throw a pound of gunpowder into the fire, the result would be quite different from the effect of a thousand spits.'

It was at this point that Lord Hayes was watching the two from his front door. Eva stopped suddenly in her walk, and spread out her hands, stretching her arms out.

'That's what I want,' she said. 'I want to develop and open. I fully believe the world is very interesting, but I am like a blind man being told about a sunset. It conveys nothing to me. And I don't believe that fifty million Sunday schools and mothers' meetings would do it for me. It must touch me somehow else. Religion and philanthropy are not the keys. I long to find out what the keys are.'

'It's a pity you don't want to marry,' said Percy.

'How do you know I don't want to marry?'

'You've told me so yourself, plenty of times. You said only a few weeks ago that you thought all men most uninteresting.'

'Yes, I know. But I'm not so egotistical as not to suspect that the fault is mine. I don't know any men well, except you, and I don't think that you are at all uninteresting. If only I could be certain—'

Eva broke off suddenly, but Percy asked her what she wished to be certain about.

'If I could be certain that I was right—right for me, that is—certain that for me life and men and women were quite uninteresting, I don't think I should mind so much. I would cease thinking about it altogether. I might even teach in the Sunday school. If all things are uninteresting, I may as well do that, and cease to expect interest in anything.'

'But aren't you conscious of any change in yourself?' asked Percy; 'and doesn't the very fact that you are getting more and more conscious that everything is very dull go to prove it?'

'I don't quite understand.'

Percy looked vaguely about, mentally speaking, for a parallel, and his eyes, sympathetically following his mind, lighted on an autumn-flowering bulb, which was just beginning to push its juicy, green spike above the ground.

'There,' he said, 'are you not, perhaps, like what that bulb was three days ago? If it were conscious it would have felt, not that it was growing, but that the earth round it was pressing it more

closely. Perhaps you are on the point of sprouting. It couldn't have known it was sprouting.'

Eva stood thinking for a moment or two.

'What an excitement it must be, after having
seen nothing but brown earth and an occasional
worm all your life, suddenly to come out into the
open air and see other plants and trees and sky.
If I am sprouting, I hope the sky will be blue
when I see it first.'

'I expect grey sky and rain makes the bulb
grow quicker.'

'Oh! but I don't care what is good for me,' said
Eva; 'I only care for what is interesting. Otherwise, I should have done all sorts of salutary things
all my life—certainly a great number of unpleasant things; one is always told that unpleasant
things are salutary.'

'I don't believe that,' said Percy: 'I think it's
one's duty to be happy.'

'Oh! but, according to the same idea, the salutary
and unpleasant things produce ineffable joy, if you
give them time,' said Eva.

They walked back to the house in silence, but
on the steps Eva stopped.

'Perhaps you're right, Percy,' she said; 'perhaps I am sprouting, though I don't know it. Certainly I feel more and more confined by all these dull days than I used to. I wonder what the world will look like when I get above ground. I hope you are right, Percy; I want to sprout.'

'It is such a comfort to think that no crisis ever fails to keep its appointment,' said he. 'When one's nature is prepared for the crisis, the crisis comes. Anything will do for a crisis. It is not the incident itself that makes the difference, but the change that has been going on in one-self.'

'Yes, that's quite true. It is no use wanting a crisis to come, or thinking that one is ready for it, if one only had a chance. If one really is ready for it, anything is a crisis. People who get con-verted, as they think, by hearing a hymn sung, think it is the hymn that has done it, and they don't realise that it is what has been going on in themselves first. Anything else would do as well.'

For the next few days all Eva's surroundings combined to strengthen her already existing bias. Percy went away; her father was more stern and exacting than usual; her mother, Eva felt, was watching her, as one watches a barometer the day before a picnic, and tapping her to see whether she was inclining to fine weather or stormy. Moreover, the little talk she had had with Percy strengthened her desire to see and judge the world. Perhaps she would always find it uninteresting. If that was so, the sooner she knew it the better; but the probability was strongly against it, and if it was not uninteresting to the core, she was simply wasting time. These August days were more tedious than ever; she read novels, but they bored her; she tried to paint, but got tired of her picture almost before she had drawn it in; all the neighbours—and there were not many of them — seemed to be away. Lord Hayes's apparently was the only house open, and of him she naturally saw nothing.

It was four days after Percy's departure that Lord Hayes came to call. Eva was sitting on the lawn behind the house when he arrived; she saw him coming out through the open French window in the drawing-room, and down the little iron staircase. She rose to meet him, and told the footman to bring tea out. Her choice, she knew, was imminent, and she

had one momentary impulse to stop him, to give herself more time, but the instant afterwards the other
picture rose before her—that flat perspective of level
days, a country without hill or stream, her own life
at home, and, on the other hand, the possibilities of
her new sphere—the world and all it contained. Was
this man, perhaps, the owner of the key which would
unlock it all to her?   Among other men she ranked
him high, perhaps the highest ; he had never pestered
her, or stared at her as if she was a picture ; he had
never bored her ; perhaps he understood her need ;
perhaps he could supply it.

They shook hands, and stood there for a moment
silent.   Then he said,—

'You promised to show me your beautiful garden.
I can see it like a jewel among the trees from
Aston.'

'Yes; the flowers are very bright just now,' she
said, speaking naturally.   'Let us go down the
terrace.'

At the bottom of the terrace he stopped. The
cedar hid them from the house, and they were alone.

'Your father told me I might call here,' he said,
'and tell you why I have come.'

Eva was standing about three feet off him, with her hands clasped behind her. He made a step forward.

'Eva, you know—'

Still she made no sign.

'I have come to ask you whether you care for me at all—whether you will be my wife?'

'I will be your wife,' she said, without smiling but letting her hands drop down by her side.

He took one of her disengaged hands in his, and bent forward to kiss it. She looked at him steadily, as if questioning him—and the long perspective of level days had passed from her life for ever.

CHAPTER III

THE account of Eva's wedding, the description of her dress, the dramatic tears which Mrs Grampound shed as her daughter was led to the altar, the size of the celebrated family diamonds, are not these things written in the *Morning Post?* And as they are recorded there, by pens better fitted than mine to do honour to the glories of the old embroidery on Eva's train, the Valenciennes lace on her dress, the tulle, the pearls, the white velvet and all the unfading splendours of the matrimonial rite, I will merely say that everything was performed on a scale of the utmost magnificence, that two princes were there, and several dukes, one of whom was heard remark out loud in church : ' By gad ! she's exquisite;' that another exalted personage replied, ' Lucky fellow, Hayes;' that the wife

of the exalted personage fixed her lord with a stony
stare and said ' Sh-sh-sh-sh ; ' and that he, in spite
of his strawberry leaves and his pedigree and his
frock coat, trembled in his patent leather shoes, and
in his confusion was vividly impressed with the idea
that his prayer-book consisted entirely of the service
for the visitation of those of riper years, to be used
at sea on the occasion of the Queen's accession. As
these portentous facts are not recorded in the *Morning Post*, I have thought fit to mention them here,
with one other little detail that escaped the vigilance
of the newspaper reporters. It was merely that the
bride smiled when she was asked whether she would
love, honour and obey her husband. But she
promised to do so in a firm, clear voice ; so, of course,
it was all right.

And now two months had passed, and the
newly-married pair had emerged from those bliss-
ful weeks of solitude, which are designed to make
them more used to their happiness, to help them
to realise that nothing can come between them
but death, that they have awoke from what seemed
a dream and found that it was true, that a new
life has begun for them, and that the gates

of Paradise are henceforward going to stand permanently open.

They had been to the Riviera, where Lord Hayes had bought a large, white umbrella, under which he used to smoke innumerable cigarettes and go little strolls along the beach, sometimes with Eva, but oftener alone. Eva quite fulfilled all the requisites he had wished for in a wife; she was dignified, rather silent, more than presentable. It pleased him that crowds should stand and stare at his wife as she walked up and down the fashionable promenades at Monte Carlo, in her still scornful beauty, with her deep, unregarding eyes wearily unconscious of their scrutiny; that the magnates of the earth should stand by her chair, as she lounged the southern afternoons away, indolently indifferent to the gay chatter round her. She used to play sometimes at the Casino, with the same air of utter *ennui*; though, at times, when the luck went heavily in her favour or against her, her eye would brighten. She played by no system whatever. 'If I had a system,' she said, 'the game would cease to interest me; by the doctrine of probabilities, my losses or gains would be slight if

I stuck to the same number; in fact, in the long run, it would diminish the element of chance almost to nothing. But to me the whole point of the game lies in the utter uncertainty of it; just the blind rolling of that ball, the momentum of which no one knows, not even the man who sets it rolling.'

On two occasions she laughed out loud at the tables. The first of these occasions was when she had been staking wildly on any number that happened to occur to her, and she had won, by almost miraculous luck, six times in succession. The other occasion was when she had lost ten times that sum, in a few minutes, by always betting on the same number. She liked the sensation of measuring herself with infinite and immeasurable forces, as exhibited in the laws of gravity and momentum.

But Lord Hayes had made, as the reader will have perceived, one grand mistake. He had wanted a presentable, dignified and reserved wife, a wife who was not silly, who did not simper or smirk, and he had got her. But what he had not recognised was that such characteristics do not make up a woman's soul, but are only one expression of it

under certain circumstances, and that the soul that
expressed itself in such a way was capable of ex-
pressing itself differently under other circumstances;
that all these may only be the natural and legitimate signs of a want of development, and that they
give no hint whatever as to what form that development will take, or what the developed soul will be.
In the month of June you may see everywhere, on
chestnut trees, certain compact pyramids of folded
buds, slightly glutinous to the touch. If you take
one of these off a hundred chestnut trees, you will
be unable to detect the least difference between
them. But two months later, three-quarters of those
chestnut trees are covered with spires of white
blossoms, and one quarter with spires of red—*Fabula
narratur.* But the presumption was that any given
one would be white? Certainly; but it is well to
remember that a certain number will be red.

Once or twice, then, Eva had shown, as it were, the
first hint of a coming blossom, which, somehow, was
strangely disconcerting to her lord; it was not quite
the fair white blossom he had led himself to expect.
Certain of these little episodes will be worth re-
cording.

They had spent ten days at Mentone, among other places, and had met there a certain Mr Armine, a young man of about thirty-two, of charming appearance and manner, who was amusing himself abroad for a month or two, while an army of contractors, builders and decorators were making his father's country house, to which he had succeeded by that gentleman's death, into a place more fitting for a fashionable young man to spend half the year in. He knew Lord Hayes rather well, and was quite willing to advance to the same degree of intimacy with his wife. Everyone called him Jim, for no better reason apparently than that his name was Plantagenet, but that, after all, was reason enough.

Eva had received this heavily-gilded youth with some cordiality, and he was clever enough to take advantage of it without subjecting the silver cord to too severe a strain. The silence and apathy of a Grecian-browed, velvet-eyed divinity is construed in quite a different manner to the interpretation put on the identical phenomena when exhibited by podgy though admirable members of the same sex. It is quite impossible to imagine that behind the Grecian brow, lurk thoughts that are not distinguished by the same magnificence as their frontlet.

In other words, Eva's silences, her long glances over the weary, blue horizon, her indifference to those round her, challenged conjecture, and roused eager interests, which the vivacity and attractiveness of other women might quite have failed to awaken.

Jim Armine began by finding immense pleasure in watching her beauty, as he might have watched a Greek statue, but in a few days his mere æsthetic pleasure in looking at her had dwindled to insignificance beside the fascination of something apart from her mere beauty. In those few weeks of married life, an essential change had come over her; her soul had awakened with throbs of surprised indignation, and it found its expression in a gathered intensity of indifference in her husband's presence.

She had no need to ask him why he had married her; the sense of his possession of her made itself felt as an insult and an outrage. She felt she had been duped, deceived, hoodwinked. The consciousness that she was his was like an open wound. She had sacrificed all her undeveloped possibilities to a loveless owner; all she had was no longer hers. Truly the red flowers were very different from the white.

To another man who was something of an observer, the signs of this which appeared on the surface, as the surface of dark water heaves and is stirred mysteriously and massively when the depths are moved, were profoundly interesting. The full import of this stirring, of course, he did not, could not, guess. All he knew was, that this admirably beautiful woman had moods as profound as they were mysterious; he was pre-occupied with her, interested, fascinated.

They were sitting together on the verandah of the Beau Site one afternoon, in the enjoyment of the bright, winter sun. Lord Hayes had departed with his white umbrella, to see about the purchase of a small villa which was for sale, and which stood high and pleasantly among the olive woods.

They had been for a sail in the morning, and Eva said to herself that she was tired and would stop at home. She did not trouble to make any excuse at all to her husband. He had mentioned to her that he was going to see about the villa which she had admired.

'It will be a pleasant drive up there,' he had said, 'if you care to come. You said you wanted to see the villa.'

Eva had rather wanted to see the villa, but the prospect appeared suddenly distasteful to her.

'I think I shall stop at home,' she said, and left him standing on the hotel steps.

Jim Armine, it appeared, was going to stop at home, too, and the natural consequence of this was that, half an hour later, they met on the great verandah facing south.

'This place gets stupid,' she said, seating herself in a low, basket-chair. 'I think we shall have to go away.'

'Where are you going to?' he asked.

'I had thought of Algiers; we can't go north yet. They are having blizzards in England. Besides, February in England is always intolerable.'

'I have never been to Algiers,' said Jim, pregnantly.

Eva looked at him a moment.

'Well, I suppose there's no reason why you shouldn't come with us. We haven't got a monopoly of the line.'

'I shouldn't come if you didn't want me,' he said, rather sulkily.

'Fancy asking a bride on her honeymoon whether she wanted another man with her!' she said. 'There is only one man in the moon, I've always heard.'

Poor Jim found it rather hard to keep his temper, more especially as he knew that he had nothing to complain of. He shifted his position in his chair, and fixed his eye on a sail on the horizon, so that he could see Eva without looking at her.

'Algiers is quite a model place for a honeymoon, I should think,' he said. 'Of course, the object is to get out of the world. There is too large a piece of the world at Mentone. Don't you find it so?'

Eva raised her eyebrows. This last speech seemed to her to savour of impertinence, and needed no reply. Jim was clever enough to see that he had made a mistake, and his tone altered.

'Where are you going to stay in Algiers? I believe it is pleasanter out of the town, on the hills.'

'Oh! Hayes has got a villa somewhere in Mustapha Supérieure. He has a passion for villas. He
has a strong sense of possession. We have been
making a sort of triumphal progress. He has a
villa at Biarritz, which we stayed in, and now he
has bought one here. Personally, I prefer a hotel ;
but, of course, villas are more suitable to honey-
moons. You are more alone there. But they are
rather spidery affairs if they are never lived in.'

'Oh! spiders belong to the class of idyllic insects,'
said Armine. 'They swarm in hayfields on Sunday
evenings, which is one of the most recognised
idyllic settings.'

'I don't think I can be idyllic,' remarked Eva.
'I never want to sit in hayfields. They make
one feel creepy, and all sorts of strange things
crawl down your back. It may be idyllic, but
the consciousness of the creepy things makes one
want to go for the idylls with a broom. Besides,
spiders are so like a certain class of odious men.'

Jim recalled at that moment a little thing that
had struck his attention the same morning. Lord
Hayes had been breakfasting in the verandah on
the usual continental breakfast—a couple of rolls,

two pieces of creamy butter, coffee, and a saucer of honey. A fly had found its way into the honey, and Hayes had extracted it with the butt end of his teaspoon. There was a methodical eagerness about this action that had made Jim think at that moment of a spider disentangling a fly from its web, and at Eva's words the scene flashed up before him again.

'I think I know what you mean,' he said, feeling his way.

Eva, too, had noticed the scene in the morning, and Jim's remark made her wonder whether he also had it in his mind. When she had compared spiders to an odious class of men, she had not in the least thought of her husband. The possible impertinence of his first remark received some confirmation. She was willing to be like a spider, too, if necessary.

'I daresay you do,' she said. 'There is nothing very subtle about it. I remember thinking this morning that you looked so like a spider when you were helping that fly out of your honey. Not that you belong to the odious class of men.'

Jim flushed. The whip tingled unpleasantly on his shoulders.

'It was your husband who rescued the fly out of his honey,' he said.

'Was it?' asked Eva, negligently. 'I thought it was you.'

She did not feel angry with him. He had made a mistake and had been punished for it. Justice had been done.

'It's getting rather cold,' she went on. 'Take me for a stroll, and give me your arm if you care for convention as little as you say you do. I am a little tired.'

They walked up and down the gay street in front of the hotel for half-an-hour or so. Eva felt a vague stimulus in the homage of this presentable young man, in spite of his slight awkwardnesses. She felt he was not a man whom it was easy to make a fool of, but she was making a some-what complete fool of him, and it pleased her. For the first time, perhaps, she caught a glimpse of her own power as a beautiful and attractive woman. That glimpse roused no vanity in her, but considerable interest. The sense of personal power is always pleasant; no man or woman who is alive, in any sense of the word, will acquiesce in being a unit among units, or will fail to feel a delicate growing love of power. We brought nothing into the world, and we shall assuredly take nothing out ; but while we are in the world, how we cling, with a persistence that no creed will shake, to the passionate desire for more and more and more. Eva was, in fact, on the threshold of the house called 'Know Thyself.' It is a house of varying size. To her it appeared large and well furnished.

They walked along the sea-wall westwards, and Eva sat down on the low balustrade. The air was still and windless, and forty feet below lay the smooth, grey backs of the rocks shining with the salt water.

'What a frightful coward one is,' she said, 'not to throw oneself down and see what happens next. I always flatter myself that I'm brave; but I am not brave enough to risk anything, really. I think a year ago I might have thrown myself down if it had occurred very strongly to me, because I had nothing to risk. But now things are beginning to be interesting. I should risk a certain amount of amusement and pleasure if I just stepped over that

wall. I wish you would step over and see, Mr
Armine ; only that would be no good, you couldn't
come and tell me about it afterwards.'

' Of course, lots of things are a bore,' said he,
' but I can't imagine any existence where that
wouldn't be the case. I couldn't frame a life in
my mind where one wouldn't be bored.'

' Well, I sympathise with you. I probably am
incapable—in fact, I know I am incapable—of many
emotions, but I feel bored no longer. I used to feel
nothing else.'

Armine was sitting near her, looking the other
way.

' What emotions can't you feel ? ' he asked suddenly.

Eva laughed.

' Oh ! plenty, and perhaps the most important of
all. That is why I fully expect not to feel all the
emotions that Algiers should inspire in me.'

Armine thought this remark much less inconse-
quent than it sounded, but he kept his reflections
to himself.

Two days afterwards, Eva and her husband left
Mentone for Marseilles. Jim walked down with

them to the station, accounting for his action by
saying that he expected a box from England, and
it had not arrived, though it was two days overdue.
To Eva this appeared the most shallow and unnecessary of subterfuges. There was some slight delay
in starting, and he stood by their carriage window
with his arms on the sill until the train moved.

Eva was leaning back in her corner, talking slowly
but somewhat continuously.

'I hope your box will have come,' she was saying
with fine cruelty. 'You must have been very eager
about it to come down through these dusty streets,
when you might be having a sail. I really thought
you were coming to see us off till you explained
about the box. I think I should have been rude
enough to ask you to stop at home if it had been so.
I hate being seen off. There is never anything to
say; you feel as if you ought to make pretty little
farewell speeches, but the farewell speeches always
hang fire, I notice. And no one can continue an
ordinary, rational, desultory conversation with fifty
engines screaming at him. It is much better for
everyone to pretend they are not going till the last
moment, and then jump up quickly, say good-bye,

E

and bundle into the cab. But at a railway station it is impossible to pretend you are not going. The apparatus of going is too obvious. Everyone is fussy and stupid at a station. Ah! we are really off, are we? Good-bye! I wish you were coming with us.'

Eva smiled rather maliciously. The first impertinent remark had been settled with now, and they were quits again.

Jim Armine stood on the platform watching the smoke of the receding train. He made a monosyllabic remark which is not worth setting down, and went back to the hotel. The box which he was expecting might languish alone in the parcel office for all that he cared.

The bridal pair crossed in one of the French Transatlantique steamers, which are built long and narrow for the sake of speed, and the accurate observation of the effect of a cross sea. Eva, with her serene immunity from human weaknesses, was sitting near the bows of the vessel, enjoying the warm, winter sun, and watched the great heaving masses of water, rushing up against the side of the vessel, with a sympathetic gladness in their glorious unrestraint. The position presented itself in a somewhat different

light to her husband, who retired, under the influence
of the same glorious unrestraint, with anything but
sympathetic gladness in his heart. Eva felt a little
contemptuous pity for him, but enjoyed being alone.
It was drawing near that supreme hour when the
sun just touches the horizon of water, and the depth
of colour in southern sea and sky grows almost
unbearable in its cruel fulness, in its air of knowing
something, of being able to tell one, if one could
only hear its message, some mystery that would
make things plain. Eva was sitting on the windward
side of the vessel, looking west, and her eyes were
filled with a still, questioning wonder. She had
arrived at that most agonising stage of feeling sure
that a mystery was there, without grasping what it
was to which she wanted any answer. Her mind
was full of a vague wonder and expectancy—the
wonder and expectancy of a mind just awakened
from its dreamless sleep of indifference. One arm
was thrown back, and her hand grasped the taffrail
to steady herself. She had taken off her hat, and
her hair was blown about in the singing breeze. The
human interest which had begun to dawn in her
which had stirred and woke from its sleep with a

sudden, startled cry, a few weeks ago, would not let
the other wonder slumber. The sense of the eternal
mystery of things watched side by side with the
sense of the eternal mystery of men. But for this
half-hour she was alone with it ; she was unconscious
of the heaving and tossing of the vessel; all she knew
was that she questioned, with something like passionate eagerness, the great walls of wine-dark water with
their heraldry of foam, the hissing monsters that
rose and fell round her, the luminous miracle that
was sinking in the west.

In the meantime, Lord Hayes had got, so to
speak, his second wind, had emerged from the
privacy of his cabin, and was walking along the
deck towards her with a battered, dishevelled air.
The punctuation of his steps was rigidly but irregu-
larly determined by the laws of gravity as exhibited
by a vessel pitching heavily in a fluid medium.
Eva had not seen him coming, and he stood by her
a few moments in silence.

'I feel a little better,' he remarked at length, in
precise, well-modulated tones.

Eva started and frowned as if she had been struck.
She turned on him with angry impatience.

' Ah, you have spoiled it all,' she cried.

She looked at him a moment, and then broke out into a mirthless laugh. He had wrapped a grey shawl round his shoulders, and on his head was a brown, deerstalker cap.

' My dear Hayes,' she said, ' you are in vivid contrast with the sunset, and you startled me. I was thinking about the sunset. However, it is nearly over now. You look like a sea-sick picture of twilight. That grey shawl is very twilighty. Come into the saloon and get me some tea.'

That gentleman was in too enfeebled a condition to feel resentment, even if he had been by nature resentful. It is notorious that certain emotions of the mind cannot exist under certain conditions of the body. No normal man feels a tendency to anger after a good dinner, or a tendency to patience in the ten minutes preceding that function. No one feels spiritually exalted in the middle of the morning, or heroic when suffering from slight neuralgia, and I venture to add that no one has spirit enough to feel resentful after an hour or two of sea-sickness.

The villa at Algiers was a charming, Moorish house, with a predominance of twisted pilasters and

shining tiles, and bold, purple-belled creepers flaunt-
ing it over the white walls.   It stood on the hills of
Mustapha Supérieure, above the Eastern-looking town,
surrounded by a rich, melodious garden, where the
winter nightingales sang in the boughs of orange
groves, which were bright with flower and fruit together, and where tall, listless eucalyptus trees shed
their rough, odorous fruits thick on the path. But
this soft beauty suited Eva's mind not so well as
the bold, golden sun dropping into a wine-dark sea ;
in fact, she cordially detested the place.   How much
of her hatred was due to the fact that she was alone
with her husband she did not care to ask herself.
Certainly, the even monotony of one face, one low,
well-modulated voice, was displeasing to her.

She found a malicious pleasure in giving him sur-
prises.   Her freshly-awakened interest in the human
race sometimes took the bit in its teeth and ran riot,
and, when it ran riot in his presence, she took no care
to check it, but talked in a voluble, rather vicious
vein, that startled him.   For instance, at dinner one
day, she had discussed certain books which he did
not know women even read, and announced, somewhat vividly, views on life and being which were

scarcely conventional. After dinner, they had sat out in the little passage that ran round the open square in the centre of the house, supported on twisted pillars, and Eva continued her newly-found confession of faith.

'Men seem to expect that women should be sexless replicas of themselves,' she said. 'All they would allow them is the inestimable privilege of being good. Virtue is its own reward, they say— so they cultivate their own pleasure with a fine disregard of virtue, and a curious pride in performing actions which certainly will lay up for them no store of virtuous and ineffable joy, while to the women they say; "Be good; here is a blank cheque on the bank of Providence. The bigger the better. *Au revoir.*" A delightfully simple arrangement.'

Lord Hayes gave a little cough, and added sugar to his coffee.

'I should always wish,' he said, with the air of an after-dinner speaker; 'I should always wish women to fulfil to the uttermost their own duties, which none but women can do.'

'The duty of being good,' said Eva. 'Exactly so.'

'I fail to see the justice of your remarks about the tendencies of men to regard women as sexless replicas of themselves,' he said. 'The province of women is quite different from that of men.'

'Ah! let me explain,' said Eva. 'Men are bad and good mixed. Whether the bad or the good predominates is beside the point. Leave out the bad, and introduce no vivid good, and you get the sexlessness, and what remains is a sexless goodness, which is, as I say, the sexless replica of the man. That is a man's woman.'

'No doubt it is my own stupidity,' said Lord Hayes, politely, 'but I still fail to agree with you. You do not take into account what I ventured to call the province of women, which, I say again, is quite different from the province of men.'

'*Da capo*,' murmured Eva. 'Let us agree to differ, Hayes. I am rather sleepy; I think I shall go to bed.'

Lord Hayes lighted a candle for her, and waited till it had burned up.

'Good-night,' said Eva, nodding at him.

He bent forward to kiss her, and, as before, she surrendered her face to be kissed.

The length of these episodes calls for an apology, but there is just this to be said. Life, for most of us, consists of episodes, of interruptions, of parentheses. We can few of us keep up the epic vein and go sublimely on, building up from great harmonious scenes a great harmonious whole. The scene-shifter perspires and tugs at his mighty cardboard trees and impossible castles in the forest; they are stiff, they will not turn round. And he sits down—does this irresponsible and wholly unbusiness-like scene-shifter—and meditates. After all, is life really surrounded by these giants of the theatrical forest? Do we go into remote and virgin woods and chant our love in irreproachable epics? When we have made our great scene, when we stand in the pure, unselfish, heroic, villain-massacreing, devoted climax of our existence, are we quite sure that some one will throw the ethereal oxy-hydrogen light on to us at the right moment? Will the audience recognise how great we are; and, even if they do, will not the slightest accident with the oxy-hydrogen light turn our climax into an anti-climax? The irresponsible scene-shifter begins to see a more excellent way. Roll off your forest trees ; send the manager of the oxy-hydrogen light home, give him eighteenpence to get drunk on—he will like it better than your heroic vein— let us have no scenery even. Just a few chairs and tables, a plain, grey sky, and no heroics. A few little episodes dealing of men who are not saints or silver kings, a few women who are not abbesses or Portias, who are in no epic mood, but in the mood of the majority of weak, unsatisfactory, careless, human beings, who can be unselfish and pure, but who are at times a little uncertain about the big riddle, unscrupulous, unkind, worldly. Besides, we are only in the first act at present. Perhaps the gigantic forest trees and the white light will come on later, but we do not promise. The irresponsible scene-shifter is right. So much, then, in praise of episode.

To return from the point at which we started before these unconscionable episodes found their way into the text, the honeymoon was over, the month was April, and Lord and Lady Hayes had returned to England. They were to spend a few days at Aston, and, after Easter, to go straight up to London. Old Lady Hayes was staying with her niece, who had married a certain Mr Davenport, and had one son. Reggie Davenport was a favourite with the dowager, who bullied him incessantly, and who sometimes got furious, because he never lost his temper with her. She was to spend a fortnight in London with the Hayes, as a great concession, in order to make Eva's acquaintance, and would join them as soon as they had settled. It may be stated at once, that she regarded her son's marriage as a most unprincipled and selfish act, and as an insult levelled directly at herself.

Mrs Grampound came up to see her daughter on the first day after their arrival.

'Your father would have come with me,' she explained, ' but he and Percy are away. I am quite alone at home. You are looking wonderfully well, dear, and I'm sure I needn't ask you whether you are happy.'

'Of course,' said Eva, 'those are the things that are taken for granted.'

'I've come to have a little cosy talk with you,' said Mrs Grampound, settling herself in a chair and taking off her gloves.

A cosy little soliloquy would perhaps have been a more accurate description. She wandered on in a sort of pious intoxication at the contemplation of her daughter.

'The mistress of a great house like this has very great responsibilities, my darling,' she said. 'If dear James were not such a thoroughly able and upright man, I confess I should feel a wee bit nervous at seeing my darling whirled away into such a circle. Be very sure exactly how you are going to behave. There seems to me something very beautiful in the life of all those dear, last-century, great ladies, whose husbands used to treat them with such charming old-fashioned courtesy, and lock them up whenever they went away, which must have been most tedious. Yes, and send a servant to tell the groom of the chambers to ask my lady if she would receive him. Dear me, yes.'

'I don't think Hayes means to lock me up whenever he goes away,' said Eva. 'We haven't got a groom of the chambers, either.'

'No, dear,' said Mrs Grampound; 'I was just saying, wasn't I? that all that was changed. Hus-

bands lounge in their wives' boudoirs now, and
smoke cigarettes there. So much more human
and natural. You don't mind the smell of smoke,
do you, dear?'

'On the contrary,' said Eva; 'I smoke myself.'

'Gracious, how shocking! What a wicked child.
Of course, there's no harm in it, dear; lots of
nice women smoke. I should not let Hayes know
that. When a difficult time comes—there will be
difficult times, of course, my Eva—there is no rose
without its thorns— Let me see, what was I saying—ah! yes, those little indulgences, like letting
a husband have a cigarette in the drawing-room
every now and then, are very much appreciated.
A little womanly tenderness,' continued Mrs Grampound, getting rather breathless, and volubly elo-
quent, 'a little tact, a little wifely sympathy, just
a look, the "I know, I know," which women can
put into one little look, is all that is required to
make those difficulties real advantages—concealed
facilities, one might really call them; real renewals
of the marriage vow; the rough places shall be
plain, in fact, if we may use those words.'

'We get on admirably together,' said Eva; 'he is most considerate for me, and most kind.'

'I declare I positively love him,' cried her mother. 'Of course, in any case, I should teach myself—should compel myself—to love the man of your choice, but the first time I saw him, I said to myself, that is the husband for my Eva. It was one June evening,' continued Mrs Grampound with an impressional vagueness, 'and we were dining somewhere, I can't remember where, and he was there too; dear me, I recollect it all as clearly as if it was yesterday. I remember old Lady Hayes telling us all that brown sherry was rank poison, and that she would as soon think of drinking a glass of laudanum. We all laughed a great deal, because our host had very famous brown sherry.'

'It must have been very pleasant,' said Eva.

'Dear old Lady Hayes,' said Mrs Grampound; 'such a wonderful woman, such strong, shrewd common sense; I wonder if she will go on living with you, Eva? I don't think it's a very good plan myself—there is sure to be some little unpleasantness now and then.'

' In spite of her strong, shrewd common sense?' asked Eva.

' Dear child, how you catch one's words up! Of course, her presence would be invaluable to you, if she stopped, and with such a guest constantly by you, of course you would learn a great deal. But I should make it quite plain what your relative positions must be. You are the mistress of the house, Eva; she is your husband's pensioner. Be very kind, very courteous, but very firm. Your rights are your rights. I daresay she will go to live at Brighton or Bournemouth or Bath, all those watering-places begin with a B; no doubt she has money of her own. You didn't think of asking Lord Hayes what would be done about that, did you, Eva? You might suggest it very gently and feelingly some time soon. Of course, you needn't express any opinion till you see what she is likely to do. Then, if it appears that she is proposing to live with you, just say very quietly that you will be very glad to have her. That will show, I think, that you know and are ready to insist on her occupying her proper position in the house. And you went to Algiers, did you not?'

continued her mother; 'that dear, white town set like a pearl and all that on the sapphire sea. I forget who said that about it, but it seems to me a very poetical description. I could almost find it in my heart to envy you, dearest.'

'Yes, it's a very pretty place,' assented Eva.

'Darling, why do you tell me so little?' said Mrs Grampound, more soberly. 'I have been thinking so continuously about you all the time you have been away; you have lived in all my thoughts. I have said to myself, "Eva will be at home in four weeks, three weeks, two days, one day; to-day I shall see my dearest again."'

'What is there to tell you,' said Eva, slowly. 'You assume I am happy, and I don't deny it. I am also amused and interested. I find things very entertaining. If you like I will show you some photographs of Mentone and Algiers. I lost two thousand francs at Monte Carlo. Hayes is very generous about money matters, and he has the further requirement of being very rich. He is bent on my being magnificent, and so, for that matter, am I. You shall see some fine things. I have, as you told me before my marriage, great natural advantages in the way of beauty. Diamonds suit me very well, and I have quantities of diamonds.'

Poor Mrs Grampound's mental intoxication was passing away rapidly, leaving behind a feeling of depression. At no time did her thoughts present themselves to her with distinctness; they were like seaweeds waving about close to the surface of the water. Sometimes, after a big wave had passed, sundry little ends of them appeared above the sea for a second or two, and Mrs Grampound made anxious little grabs at these before they disappeared again. Consequently, her descriptions of them, as reflected in her conversation, were somewhat scrappy and inorganic.

She appeared, in the short silence that followed Eva's remarks, to have got hold of a new sort of seaweed—a bitter, prickly fragment. At any rate she said, somewhat piteously,—

'Eva, Eva, tell me you are satisfied. You don't blame me, do you, for urging it on you?'

Eva could be very cruel. The foam-born Aphrodite, when she came 'from barren deeps to conquer all with love,' had, we may be sure, many undesirable suitors, and to these, I expect, she did not show

F

any particular kindness or sympathy. She was, to judge by her face, too divine to be cruel in petty, irritating ways, but she was too divine not to be very human.

Eva raised her eyebrows.

'Why should I blame you? I am amused and interested. After all, that is more important than anything else. Surely I ought to be grateful to you. But, to speak quite frankly, I did not marry to please you; I married to please myself, and Hayes, of course,' she added.

Mrs Grampound was very nearly shedding a few vague tears, but the appearance of Lord Hayes made her decide to postpone them.

'My charming mother-in-law,' he said, 'I am delighted to see you. Very much delighted, in fact. And am I not to see my father-in-law? How do you think Eva is looking?'

'Eva is looking wonderfully well,' said she, brisken-ing herself up a little. 'She has been giving me the most delightful accounts of your honeymoon. Mentone, Algiers, all those charming, romantic places. But Monte Carlo! Really, I was shocked. And Eva tells me she lost two hundred thousand francs

—or was it two thousand, Eva? In any case, it is quite shocking, and I feel I ought to scold you for leading my child into bad ways.'

' He didn't lead me,' said Eva. ' I went by myself. I think you remonstrated, didn't you, Hayes? You didn't play yourself, I know. However, I got a good deal of fun out of it. It was really exciting sometimes. After all, that is the chief thing. Two thousand francs was cheap. Tell mother about the new villa. I must go—I've got a hundred things to do.'

Old Lady Hayes also made inquiries of her son as to what was to happen to her. She was a direct old lady, and she said,—

' And what is to become of me?'

Lord Hayes quailed under these unmasked batteries, and felt most thankful that he would not have to meet them alone any longer. He had great confidence in Eva's courage, and felt that she would be quite up to the mark on such occasions. But he had, for the present, to trust to his own forces, and, with the idea of making the scene as little unpleasant as possible, he replied,—

' Of course, dear mother, you will do whatever

suits you best.   Your position in the house will necessarily be somewhat changed.'

' Necessarily,' said Lady Hayes.

Her son found no pertinent reply ready.

CHAPTER IV

THERE is something peculiarly substantial and English about those houses which our aristocracy brighten with their presence, in the more fashionable parts of London, during several months of the year. Those lords of the earth, who cannot manage to breathe unless they have a thousand or more acres round their houses in the country, being sensible folk, are content to live, shoulder by shoulder, in rows of magnificent barracks, when they are in London. A porch supported by Ionic pillars, with a line of Renaissance balustrade along the top, a sprinkling of Japanese awnings, a couple of dozen large, square windows looking out on to what is technically known as 'the square garden,' partly because it is round, and partly because it is sparsely planted with sooty, stunted bushes, scattered about on what courtesy interprets to be

8

grass, and surrounded by large, forbidding railings, are the characteristics of the best London houses. They may not be distinguished by any striking, artistic beauty, but they are eminently habitable.

Along one of these rows, one June afternoon, a smart victoria was being driven rapidly. It was hung on the best possible springs, and the wheels were circumscribed with the best possible india-rubber tyres. A water-cart had just passed up the street, and the air was full of that indescribable freshness which we associate in the country with summer rain, and which, in London, makes us feel that art is really doing a great deal to rival Nature. The progress of the well-appointed victoria was therefore as free from noise, jolts and dust as loco-motion is permitted to be in this imperfect world. There was only one occupant of this piece of per-fection—for, of course, the coachman and footman are part of the carriage—and she was as perfect as her equipment. In other words, Lady Hayes was going home to tea.

The carriage drew up with noiseless precision at the curb-stone, and Lady Hayes remained appar-ently unconscious of the stoppage till the powdered

footman had rung the bell, and turned back the
light crimson rug that covered her knees. Then
she rose languidly and trailed her skirts across the
pavement to the house. Above the porch was a
square, canvas tent, with one side, away from the
sun, open to admit the breeze, and Eva, as she
passed upstairs, said to the man standing in the
hall, 'Tea upstairs, above the porch.' This tent
opened out of a low window in the drawing-room,
through which Eva passed, and in which was sitting, as gaunt and forbidding as ever, her respected
mother-in-law. That lady had grudgingly complied
with the popular but misguided prejudices of London
with regard to the skins wherewith the human animal
clothes itself, but her stiff, black silk gown was as
awe-inspiring as her grey, Jaeger dress and the boots
with eight holes a-piece in them.

They had all been in London nearly a month, and
the excellent old lady was living in a permanent
equipment of heavy armour, with which to repel,
assault and batter her daughter-in-law. Eva, on the
contrary, despised the old methods of warfare, and
met these attacks, or led them, with no further im-
plements than her own unruffled scorn, and a some-

what choice selection of small daggers and arrows, in the shape of a studied delicacy of sarcasm and polite impertinences. She resembled, in fact, an active and accomplished pea-shooter, who successfully pelted the joints of a mature and slowly-moving Goliath. The dowager glanced up as she entered. One of her laborious mottoes was 'Punctuality is the root of virtue,' and Eva, in consequence, held the view that punctuality is the last infirmity of possibly noble minds. She was quite willing to believe that her mother-in-law had an incomparably noble mind ; she did not underrate her antagonist's strong points ; in fact, her whole system was to emphasise them.

'Ah, you've come at last,' said old Lady Hayes. 'And pray, when are we to have tea?'

'I am late,' said Eva. 'I always am late, you know. Why didn't you have tea without me? Is Hayes in?'

'The servants have quite enough to do with the dance to-night without bringing up tea twice.'

'Ah that is so thoughtful and charming of you,' said Eva, drawing off her long gloves. 'The merciful man considers his beast. That is so good of you.'

'And he considers his servants as well,' said the dowager.

'Oh! I think servants are meant to be classed as a sort of beast. The good ones are machines with volition; and if they are bad servants, of course they are beasts.'

The dowager turned over the leaves of the current number of the *Lancet* with elaborate unconsciousness.

Eva finished taking off her gloves, and whistled a few bars of a popular tune.

'I don't know if it's customary for women to whistle now-a-days,' said the old lady, for whistling, as Eva knew, was a safe draw, 'but in my time it was thought most improper.'

'Isn't there a French proverb—I daren't pronounce French before you—about "we have changed all that?" That is a very silly proverb. It is the older generation who changed it themselves. They made their own system of life impossible. They reduced it to an absurdity.'

The dowager, who spoke French with a fine Scotch accent, and knew it, finished buckling on, as it were, her greaves and cuirass, and presented arms.

'I confess I don't understand you. No doubt I am very stupid—I should like very much to know how we have reduced our life to an absurdity.'

'I don't say the modern generation are not quite as absurd,' said Eva, 'but the difference is that they have not yet learned their absurdity. You see, the whole race of men, since B.C. 4004—that is the correct date, is it not?—have been devoting themselves to the construction of any theory of life which would hold water, and one by one they have been abandoned. The new theory, that nothing matters at all, has not yet been disproved, and considering that no theory hitherto has ever been permanent, it would be absurd to abandon this one till it is disproved in as convincing a manner as all its predecessors.'

'I imagine that no previous age has ever sunk so deep in mere sensuous gratifications,' said the dowager, lunging heavily.

'Ah, do you think so?' said Eva. 'Of course, it is impertinent in me to try to argue the matter with you, as experience is the only safe guide in such matters, and you have experience of at least one more generation than I. But that seems

to me altogether untrue. As we know from the
Bible, desire shall fail, because it has been gratified
to the utmost that human desire can conceive, I
imagine. Well, I think desire has failed to a great
extent. The men of your generation, for instance,
and the generation before, drank so much port wine
that this generation drink none. The daily three
bottles that our grandfathers and great-grandfathers
indulged in, has fulfilled the desire of port to the
uttermost. No one gets drunk now. I don't think
I ever saw a man drunk. They used to fall under
the table, did they not? What a charming state of
things! But it has at least produced a fastidiousness
in us, which considers heavy drinking coarse and low.'

'My father was a teetotaler, and so was my
husband,' said the old lady, rather wildly.

'I think that the habit of drinking in men,' continued Eva, 'is really the fault of the women ; you,
of course, are an instance in point. Your husband
was a teetotaler—surely, through your influence.
If the men of the last generation were vile, the
women, I think, were viler still. What is that word ?
Oh! yes, vicarious. The men sinned vicariously for
the women.'

'It is easy to speak lightly of the virtues of your forefathers,' remarked the dowager; 'much easier than to practise them yourself.'

'Ah! you misunderstand me,' said Eva. 'Heaven forbid that I should speak lightly of them! Their virtues were as gigantic and as loathsome to them, as their vices are to me. They used to go to church with the most appalling regularity, and eat salt fish in Lent, and have their clergyman to dinner on Sunday, which meant no port wine to speak of. Of course, they made up for it by having a little quiet cock-fighting on Sunday afternoon, but you cannot expect perfection.'

'Cock-fighting seems to me no more brutal than butchering hand-reared pheasants,' said the dowager.

'Ah, that is the war-cry of people who don't know anything about shooting,' said Eva. 'The hand-reared pheasant comes over the guns at the height of about sixty feet, at forty miles an hour. I watched them shooting last year at home. There was a big wind, and Hayes missed seventeen birds in succession. Take a gun and try for yourself. Of course, you say the same thing about partridge-driving. You say the manly thing is to walk your partridges up, instead of having them driven to you. The truth is, that one of the reasons why men go partridge-driving now is because it is so much more difficult than walking them up. Certainly Hayes's butchery of hand-reared pheasants was a most humane proceeding. Did you ever see a cock-fight?'

'Cock-fighting improved the breed,' said the other, 'though I disapprove of it entirely.'

'Well,' said Eva, 'it killed off the weak ones. The survival of the fittest, of course. And we reap the benefits by having particularly large eggs to eat ; at least, I suppose a stalwart chicken begins life in a stalwart egg.'

Old Lady Hayes rose with dignity.

'I think tea must be ready,' she said. 'In fact, it is probably cold by this time.'

'Time does pass so in conversation,' said Eva, languidly. 'Ah! they have sent some orchids. How nice and cool they look.' She snapped off a spray of the delicate, cultured blossoms, and fastened them in her dress. 'I think tea is put in the room above the porch. I rather expect Jim Armine,' she

said, as she settled herself in a low, basket-chair.
'I wonder when the absurd custom of women
pouring out tea will go out; why a woman
should have that abominable trouble I cannot
think. Of course, when tea was rather a rarity,
a sort of up-to-date luxury, it was natural. The
hostess gave her guests a smart little present.'

Old Lady Hayes accepted the challenge.

'It used to be held to be the province of women
to be matronly and womanly and domestic,' she
said. 'They were in their places at the fireside,
at the tea-table, not in the smoking-room and
in grand stands.'

'I am referring to the manual labour of pouring out tea,' said Eva; 'but whatever the province
of women may be, they seem to me to fill it very
inadequately when their husbands go to bed drunk
every night. It is such a comfort to know that
your father and husband were teetotalers, for I
can say these things without their being personal.
Your father was a Presbyterian minister, was he
not? How do you call it in the dear Scotch language—meenister, isn't it?'

'He was a learned, upright man.'

'How nice!' said Eva. 'I can add a meenister to my ancestry. Do you know who my great-grandfather was? He was a crossing-sweeper, originally, in New York. Then he went West, you know, and, being 'cute, made a pile.'

'You have very distinct traces of your American origin,' said the old lady with asperity.

'And you of the dear Scotch talk,' said Eva. 'I always like the Scotch so much. They are so honest and sterling and serious. Hoots, mon!' she added meditatively.

The dowager took a second cup of tea. She had been accustomed to consider tea as a destructive agent in the days of seven o'clock dinner, but as Eva refused personally to dine till half-past eight, she found that, though perhaps destructive, it was less unpleasant than pure inanition. She had enunciated some startling warnings as to what would happen to people who dined at half-past eight earlier in her sojourn in London, and Eva had told her, with great courtesy, that she was quite at liberty to dine at seven or half-past six, or six if she liked, but she was afraid that her daughter-in-law would be unable to share the meal with her. Whether her mother-in-law's constitution had become so strongly fortified by the use of drugs that she could now afford to play tricks with it, we are not called upon to say; at any-rate, the half-past eight dinner had, at present, made no perceptible inroads on her digestive or vital powers.

Eva had finished tea, and proceeded to light a cigarette.

'After our dreadfully keen encounter,' she explained, 'I want soothing. Argument is very trying to the nerves. Tobacco, on the other hand, is eminently soothing. Permit me to soothe myself.'

Old Lady Hayes watched these proceedings through eyelids drooped over vigilant, irritated eyes.

Eva's whole personality was radically abhorrent to her. Her complete modernity seemed to her an epitome of all that is unsuitable to woman. Even her best points—her extreme tolerance, her cold purity—were repugnant, because they were the outcome of what she considered a wrong principle. Tolerance, according to the old lady's code, was the fruit of charity—Eva's tolerance was the fruit of indifferences. In the same way, the purity, the utter stainlessness of Eva's mind was the result of fastidiousness, which, according to the other, was the sinful opposite of charity. Purity *via* fastidiousness, not morality, was to her the fig on the thistle, the grape on the thorn, which, however excellent in itself, could not be good because it must partake of the nature of its parent stem.

'Of course, I know how utterly you must disapprove of me,' continued Eva with sincerity; 'my whole system, or rather want of system, of life, must seem to you to be utterly inexcusable. Life is a complicated business and rather tiresome at the best. It is continually fractious and annoying and irritating. Its whole object seems to be to make one angry. But my plan is to bear with it; to treat it as a tiresome child, not to let it irritate and annoy me, to avoid all possible collisions with it—and, to do all this, you mustn't be serious or too particular.'

' I was brought up to believe in moral responsibilities,' said the old lady, 'in some idea of duty, in a notion that it was not our mission simply to mause ourselves and disregard others.'

'Just so,' said Eva ; 'that illustrates very well what I mean by reducing things to an absurdity. Duty dominated everything, and the port wine affairs were merely regarded as interludes. Of course, if men are brought up to believe in these ponderous responsibilities, they must have interludes. We have done away, or rather you made it inevitable that we should do away, with responsibilities and interludes alike.'

'And not unnaturally you have nothing left.'

'Quite so. We are human beings who find themselves in a state of consciousness, and a state of consciousness demands that you should do something or think something. We fulfil those demands to a certain extent, but we do not make a mumbo-jumbo of them. You see there have always been a certain number of people with a desire to do certain things — to be kind, to be respectable and reasonable ; and a certain number of these have a tendency — we all have tendencies—to construct a theory about what they do. They have, to begin with, a genius for doing their duty, and doing your duty is an unremuner- ative occupation in this wicked world. Then there

comes in their inexorable need of making a theory
Duty is unremunerative here, but amusing oneself is
remunerative. Therefore there must be a place
and a time when the balance is struck, when to
have done your duty is remunerative, and not to
have done your duty is unremunerative; and the
Paradiso and the Inferno are already made.'

The blood of all the clans was up.

'Do you mean to say,' gasped the dowager,
'that you deny the existence of—'

'Ah, my dear lady,' said Eva, 'do not let us
say things we shall be sorry for afterwards. I
deny nothing, and I affirm nothing. I am only
pointing out that many people do deny and affirm
a great many things. The fault lies with them.
If they had affirmed nothing, and denied nothing,
would the fact that I did the same seem so
horrible to you? Would you have evolved all
your system of denials and affirmations out of
your own inner consciousness?'

This was a little too much. Old Lady Hayes
surged up out of her chair and confronted her.

'You believe nothing — you fear nothing — you
love nothing. All you care for, are your wretched

little hair-splittings about tendencies, and the modern
view of life. When you call my beliefs supersti-
tions and inventions, you think you have annihil-
ated them.'

'Excuse me,' said Eva, 'I have no wish to
annihilate them, nor do I pretend to do so. I
wish I shared them. It must make everything so
very easy if it is labelled right or wrong ; if every
choice is like a cross road with a sign - post,
" Heaven and Hell." It must be so like those
little allegories about children with bare feet walking along a dusty road, with flowers by the side, and
lions and tigers hiding among the flowers. Having
read the allegories, of course, you know that if you
only keep to the road, it will soon become flowery,
and beautiful boots will mysteriously grow on to
your feet. And you have the inestimable satisfaction of seeing the lions and tigers gnawing at the
bones of the people who go to pick flowers, and
of reflecting that not only do they have no beautiful boots, but that the lions and tigers have eaten
them up, so that the beautiful boots would be no
use to them even if they had them. No doubt
you expect me to be seized upon soon, and eaten.

It must be very unpleasant. I notice that you never go to help them ; you are too much occupied in walking along your tight-rope road.'

' This is mere burlesque.'

' And who is the author of this burlesque ? ' asked Eva.

' Perhaps it is another characteristic of your generation to ridicule the most sacred beliefs of others,' she replied. ' I should have thought any code of good manners would have forbade that. Jews take off their hats when they come into a Christian church.'

Eva rose without any show of haste or impatience.

' *Au revoir,*' she said. ' You will excuse me, I know. I have half-a-hundred things to do.'

She went through the open window into the drawing-room. As she passed the head of the stairs, she saw a well-known figure coming up, preceded by a footman.

' Ah, Jim,' she cried, ' how late you are. Come to my room. I have been discussing religious questions with my mother-in-law, and, well—and so we parted, in more senses than one. Have you had tea? No? Bring Mr Armine some tea to my room.'

'She's rather a powerful old lady, isn't she?' asked Jim, who, since the Hayes' return from abroad, had managed to establish himself on a fairly intimate footing.

'She has been abusing me with immense power and vigour,' said Eva. 'I am the incarnation of all that is horrible in her eyes. The one incomprehensible thing to that generation is this generation.'

'The converse holds, too,' said he.

'No; I understand them perfectly. Their nature is the basis of ours; we are the heirs of all previous ages, just as they were. The later development has incorporated the earlier, but it is contrary to the nature of the earlier to understand the later. Just in the same way, I understand what I was a year ago, though, if I saw now what I should be in another year, it would probably be incomprehensible to me.'

'I shouldn't have thought you would change much.'

Eva took a book from a small table near her, and opened it with a quick, dramatic movement.

'It is like that,' she said. 'Whether I have changed, or only discovered, I don't know. But a year ago the book was shut, and now I have read the first chapter.'

'At any rate, you have some ideas about the last chapter, then; I suppose all the characters have come on the stage?'

'Ah! but who can tell what will happen to them? No character can be uninfluenced by circumstances. If it is a book worth reading, they will have altered by the end. Circumstances have led me to open the book, they will determine my subsequent career; and circumstances, in the shape of gout or cancer or something, will make me close it.'

'Is it interesting reading?'

Eva looked at him, with a smile gathering on her mouth.

'Particularly interesting,' she said. 'I am sure you are interested too.'

In the silence that followed, a tap came at the door, which was repeated, and Lord Hayes entered. He was irreproachably dressed in a black frock coat, with a fine gardenia in his button-hole. He was rather short-sighted, and blinked in the manner of a small, tame owl.

'I am sure I beg your pardon,' he said; 'but I tapped, and there was no answer, and so I came in.'

Eva turned to him.

'It is of no consequence. Have you had tea?'

'I found some tea in the drawing-room, thank you. I am bound to say it was rather cold.'

'Have you seen your mother?'

'Yes; she was not cordial. Her manner implied that she had been a little upset about something. She is going to stay with the Davenports for a week, in Hyde Park Gardens, she said, before she goes down into the country. She has, in fact, determined to leave us on the day after to-morrow, instead of stopping till next week.'

Eva pointed to a box of cigarettes.

'You may smoke,' she said; 'Jim, the matches are by you.'

'A cigarette would be very refreshing,' said Lord Hayes. 'The heat and the noise have made me a little fatigued. And, I suppose, we shall be up very late to-night. My mother informed me she would not be present at our little dance.'

'Not even at the cotillion?' asked Eva.

'The cotillion ought to be very pretty,' said he. 'I am satisfied with the appearance of the room. I sent word to Aston not to spare the choicest orchids. Have you seen the staircase since they put the flowers in?'

'Yes,' said Eva; 'it looks charming. I am much obliged to you for taking all that trouble.'

Lord Hayes bowed.

'I am delighted,' he said. 'I am very glad you are satisfied. Princess Frederick is coming, is she not?'

'Yes,' said Eva; 'I met her this afternoon. I did not know she was in London. Of course I asked her.'

'It will be very brilliant,' said her husband, solemnly.

Jim Armine rose to go.

'You will be here to-night?' asked Eva. 'We don't begin till eleven.'

'The heat is getting very oppressive,' said Lord Hayes, politely, as he opened the door for him. 'The thermometer was standing at eighty-two degrees in the window of White's.'

Eva was sitting back in her chair, in an attitude that was common with her, with her two hands clasped over one knee. She had developed a great power of doing nothing; whether it was a survival of the days of the blank white page, or an effect of the change that had given her so much to think about, is doubtful; probably the habit of the first was adapted to the needs of the second. Life was interesting and amusing—a new book in a new language. She had found herself suddenly transplanted from a silent, pleasant garden to a crowded reception-hall. Her tastes did not lie in the direction of gardens; they seemed to her very monotonous. The beautiful but silent and weary-looking girl, who had been looked at and passed by, found London a different place when she learned that the rows of eyes in the reception-room looked to her as a sort of centre. There is nothing so inexplicable as the phenomenon called 'the rage.' The opera screamed and starved unheard for years in London, when suddenly the whole of London became aware that it was the most delicious thing in the world. It had been there all the time; it was advertised in the morning papers, but nobody cared. In the same

way with Eva—she was living before, and she was
living after; she had been advertised at balls and
concerts, but the advertisement had been entirely
unremunerative. Then a middle-aged peer had remarked that Miss Grampound seemed to him worthy
of the highest compliment that a man can pay a
woman, with the consequence that all London was
of one mind that she was exactly what they had been
looking for so long. Eva's head was not turned, nor
was her heart touched, but the effect was that she
became conscious of herself, and conscious of other
people. Pygmalion had touched Galatea and Galatea sprang to life.

Pygmalion inevitably has the worst of it. When
a whole race of men bursts almost simultaneously
on one woman, it is not to be expected that she
will single out one. They are all queer and interesting, some are attractive. Poor little Pygmalion
may beat his breast in the corner and say, ' It
is mine, it is all mine,' but no one will listen to
him; least of all Galatea. His best course is to
keep on good terms with his handiwork, and be
very polite and obliging. He is compelled to
act as bear-leader to this incarnated stone, but

he had better not allude to the time when he called her off her pedestal; and unless he is a fool, he will not try to put any finishing stroke to his handiwork. He let her have a soul, let him remember that he did not let her have it. The material is his, her flesh and blood, for he paid for it when it came from the quarries, but his possession ends there. The rest is hers and all the world's.

Lord Hayes sat down again on the chair he had just left, and repeated his remark about the thermometer at White's. Eva stifled a yawn.

'I suppose that was in the shade, was it not?'

'Oh, yes,' he said; 'in the sun the temperature would have been much higher.'

'Your mother and I had a somewhat plain-spoken conversation this afternoon,' she said; 'I came in for a good deal of abuse.'

'I imagined her sudden departure was owing to something of the kind,' he said. 'I am sorry it has occurred; personally, I always avoid quarrelling with anyone.'

'It is a mistake,' said she; 'but if two people disagree, they must quarrel some time. Besides,

I didn't quarrel with her. I was even amused, I am sorry to say.'

'That is—if you will pardon my saying so—the surest method of quarrelling.'

Eva looked at him gravely.

'You have admirable good sense,' she said ; 'I always thought you had. But, after all, it is a good thing to be amused.'

BOOK II

THERE are certain hours of the day which seem to exist only in England, and one of these is the hour before dinner in winter. We are quite certain that there is a certain time in all countries which is identical, according to the statements made by clocks and other clumsy contrivances, with this sacred time, but it is not the same thing. Where else in the world may we look for that sense of domestic comfort, that hour thought away before the fire, after a long day's tramp in the snow or an afternoon on black, patient ice, that lends itself to be drawn and scribbled on by the ringing, clear-cutting skates? The hour is there, the pitiful, unmeaning sixty minutes, from half-past six to half-past seven, but it is a mockery, a delusion, with no more soul about it than a photograph or a bust. Let us look at the real thing.

Firelight—no candles, but bright firelight—enough to think by. A chair drawn up on to the hearth-rug, and two large feet resting on the fender. If you look about, you will see two evening shoes lying near, and, if you are human, you will sympathise with the impulse that led to their temporary want of employment.

The proprietor of these large feet is proportionately large. He has half-dressed for dinner; that is to say, a rough, Norfolk jacket takes the place of a dress-coat, and he has no shoes on. He has been out shooting all day, and got a very fair bag, with twelve woodcock among it, which is truth, not grammar. When he came in, after a bitterly cold and entirely satisfactory day, he drank no less than three cups of tea and ate an alarming quantity of muffins. Then, being still very cold and ex-tremely dirty, he wallowed for a quarter of an hour in a bath about as large as a small pond, and be-came warm and clean. Then he dressed for dinner, barring the dress-coat, came into the smoking-room, where he kicked off his shoes, lit a briar-wood pipe, and proceeded to spend the next half-hour in looking at the fire, enjoying the particular peace of mind which is inseparable from a sane mind and a sane body.

While he looks into the fire and finds entertainment there, we may as well take a look at the room and then at him. It is always a good plan to look well at anyone's room, for everyone leaves on a room they frequent, a personal impress which is almost always infallible. An aquiline nose or a deep, dreamy eye are often the legitimate outcome of an ancestry with certain tendencies, which may have dropped out of existence in any particular case, though their corporeal stamp remains, but no Crusader or king of Vikings will be able to touch with their ghostly fingers the particular sanctum of any man or woman in the nineteenth century. Their portraits may frown down from the walls of the dining-hall, but the clank of their swords, the rhythm of their oars, is not heard in the smoking-room.

A table-cloth, betwixt and between the table and the floor, and half-a-dozen cartridges, which act as a drag on its slipping further, may be of too ephemeral a nature to lay much stress on, but they are indications which will be useful if borne out by confirmatory evidence. A book-case—that is better. Badminton on shooting, Badminton on hunting, Badminton on coursing, Badminton on racing, Badminton on fishing; let us not forget the six cartridges. A book upside down on the top shelf, with not more than forty pages cut—*Robert Elsmere.* Remember that. Four volumes of Dickens, bearing the mark of a well-spent and battered existence. *Tess of the D'Urbevilles*—not more than half cut, but the last six pages also cut. That also, in conjunction with the state of *Robert Elsmere,* is distinctly important. *Ravenshoe*—signs of wear—in much the same state as Pickwick. *Demosthenes' de Corona*—dog-eared and filthy, with the meanings of many unpardonably irregular Greek words, I am sorry to say, written down in the margin in a minute hand. The utterly abandoned, dishevelled appearance of the rest of the book suggested that the extreme care with which these were written was not wholly owing to any reverential adoration of that immortal author. A small Greek Lexicon, from γ to ψ inclusive, also filthy, with several crude but vivid illustrations in red ink. A volume of Browning. Certain lyrical poems, with pencil marks by the side—a difficult factor, but not in-explicable.

Such were the habits, so to speak, of this room, to which we confidently hope to find a key in the habits of the six feet something of flesh and bone warming itself in front of the fire. Making all possible allowance for the deceptive character of appearances, we may at once hazard two epithets on him—well-bred and English. In spite of the thorough tanning his skin had undergone, you would be right in concluding that he was a pure English-man, who had been subjected lately to a tropical sun ; in fact, he had only been a fortnight in England. His name, to descend to less metaphysical matters, was Reginald Davenport, the son of a Mr Davenport, who has been mentioned incidentally in this history as being the nephew, by marriage, of old Lady Hayes, and whose house the dowager had selected to be her ark of refuge, after she had been driven out, with loss, by Eva's criticisms on religion and the last genera-tion. Eva had never seen her handsome young connection, for he had been travelling for the last year, and only came back to England, as I have said, two weeks before we discovered him in the smoking-room—some five months after Eva had left London. He was a friend of Percy, Eva's brother; in fact, that gentleman was expected here this evening, to do murder and sudden death among the woodcock. And someone else was coming, who, to tell the truth, interested Reggie far more than any number of his other friends. Percy had intimated that he was in the habit of falling in love once a fortnight, and he had just done so to such good purpose that he was definitely and irrevocably engaged. These periodic fallings in love were slightly embarrassing, because the charming girls with whom he fell in love — he never fell in love with anyone who was not charming—some times fell in love with him; and the emotional atmosphere of his neighbourhood became extremely electrical and exciting.

On the whole, I feel inclined to risk another epithet in this preliminary skirmishing round Reggie. Yes—indubitably boyish. By boyish, I mean the power of enjoying life without thinking about it. Such a gift—the gift of serene receptiveness, of complete irresponsibility—is rare, fascinating and, at times, intensely irritating. The majority of ordinary work-a-day folk have, as Eva said, a certain capacity for doing their duty, and forming theories about it. Reggie knew no obscure idol called Duty, to which he owed obedience, but he was ruled by a quantity of cleanly, wholesome instincts, that made him honest, good-natured, lovable and affectionate. The worst of drawing your morality from the springs of your nature is that, if a mischievous hand gets to meddling with those springs, to diverting the course of the water, or, perhaps, putting a little piece of something not entirely wholesome in that clear fountain, your moral digestion is considerably disorganised. At the same time, an innate morality is productive of a more lively faith than a collection of dried plants from the gardens of other men's experience. They may be the same plants, but they are alive, not pressed and sapless.

Reggie never hazarded any guesses as to the answer of that Gordian riddle called life. The how, why and wherefore of existence cannot even be said to have been uninteresting to him—such questions did not exist for him at all. But, by virtue of an innate sweetness of disposition, he had an undoubted capacity for being content to live, and be nice to those in the same predicament of living as himself. Such natures are not often saddled with great mental gifts; but very often hold a great capacity for loving and being loved, with the restful love one feels for shady places on dusty roads, for the 'times of refreshing' that are so divinely human. This gift is one which many children possess, and which few retain beyond childhood. It is dangerous, fascinating, dazzling, seductive and very unsettling, but it is very sweet.

This fathom of well-bred, boyish, English life was nearly asleep, but not quite. In fact, a very slight sound made him particularly wakeful, for it was a sound for which he had been listening—the sound of carriage wheels outside. He went quickly out of the room, and was in the hall before the front door was opened. Ah! well, the meeting of two young lovers is very pretty, but it has happened before.

Percy arrived in time for dinner, and when Mr Davenport retired from the smoking-room soon after eleven, he left there the two young men, who did not seem inclined to go to bed. Reggie, in fact, had an alarming number of things to say,

and he proceeded to say them with guileless straightforwardness.

'I am awfully glad you were able to come,' he
began; 'I wanted you to see Gertrude very much.
You must be my best man, you know. We're not
going to be married yet; not for a year. You see,
I was half-engaged when I went to India, and
we settled to wait then for two years. Well,
one year's gone, that's something.'

'You're a detestably lucky fellow,' said Percy,
on whom a charmingly pretty and thoroughly nice
girl had made her legitimate impression.

'Oh! I know I am; detestably lucky, as you say.
Doesn't she sing beautifully, too? Hang it all,
I won't talk about it, or else I shall go on for ever,
and it's rather dull for you.'

Percy laughed.

'Oh, don't mind me. I'm very happy. Pour
out your joyful soul, but pass me a cigar first.'

Cigars?' said Reggie. 'I really had quite forgotten about smoking. That's what comes of being
in love. Really, old fellow, you had better fall in
love as soon as you possibly can. Depend upon
it, there's nothing like it. Here, catch!'

Reggie chucked a cigar-case across to him.

'Have you seen your new cousin yet?' asked Percy.

'Who? Oh, Lady Hayes. No, I haven't. She's perfectly lovely, isn't she?'

'Eva has always been considered good-looking,' remarked the other solemnly.

'I don't particularly care for Hayes himself,' said Reggie. 'He's so awfully polite and dried up. But I expect your sister's made him wake up a bit. I want to know her. Where is she?'

'They're abroad again, at present. Jim Armine's with them.'

'Jim Armine?' said Reggie, doubtfully. 'That pale chap with a big place in Somersetshire?'

'Probably the same. I don't know why Eva likes him so. I can't bear him.'

'He's an oily sort of fellow,' remarked Reggie, frankly. 'But lots of women like him. He's too clever for me. I'm awfully stupid, you know.'

'They met him abroad on their honeymoon,' said Percy, 'and he hung about a good deal, I fancy.'

'I'm blowed if I'll have another man hanging about on my honeymoon,' said Reggie.

'No; I don't suppose you will. It does seem one too many to the unbiassed mind. Rather like the serpent in paradise, who was certainly *de trop*.'

'What serpent?' said Reggie, who was obviously thinking of something else. 'Oh, I see, the devil, you mean.'

'No, I didn't mean the devil exactly; I meant any third person.'

'We're going shooting to-morrow over the High Croft,' said Reggie, after a pause, in which he had determined, by a rapid mental process, that he was unable to initiate any more statements on the subject of the serpent, 'and Gertrude and mother are going to bring us lunch. You and father will have to shoot alone after lunch; I'm going to drive on with Gertrude, just round about and home again.'

Gertrude Carston certainly seemed a most desir-able partner for Reggie; they were really both of them detestably lucky people. She had consider-able beauty, of a large, breezy order; she was quite as adorably child-like as he, and showed quite as few signs of any tendency to grow up. She was fond of hunting, lawn-tennis, animals, loud hymns, anything, in fact, of a pronounced and intelligible stamp; she was quite ridiculously fond of Reggie, and they both behaved in the foolish, delightful manner in which people in such a predicament do behave. They had both settled to get up early the next morning and have a short walk before breakfast, which was not till a quarter to ten, but in the morning they both felt it quite impossible to do so, and came down feebly a few minutes after the gong had sounded, and pretended that they had been up an immense time waiting for the other, till that particularly flimsy falsehood broke down, and they both laughed prodigiously. It was obviously a good, honest love-match; for each of them only the other existed, in no ethereal, mysterious form, but simply as a capital, honest human being, lovable in every part. There were no regrets, no unsatisfied longings, no sentimental, half-morbid affection that was exacting or jealous. Love, like Janus of old, is a two-headed god. On some he smiles, to others his eyes are full of strange, bewildering doubts; on his lips there's a smile that is half a sigh, that wakes at times a tumultuous happiness, a bitter aching at others, and never brings content. That love may be more complex, more worthy of the agonised questionings with which men and women have worshipped him, more deserving of the reproach, the longing, the dread, the reviling, that has found its expression in bitter verses and heart-broken epigrams, but the simple, smiling face is there for some to see, and those are blest who see it. Their love may be on a lower level, but it is very sweet, and lies among pleasant gardens, and by melodious streams; for such there is no mountain top, compassed about by heaven; earth lies about them, not beneath them, and for them there is no painful climbing, no bleeding hands or panting breasts, and perhaps, at the top, nothing but clouds and cold, palpable mist.

Such, at any rate, was their love at present, yet nothing is safe in this uncertain world. An earthquake may rend the pleasant garden, an east wind may wither its flowers, drought may drink up its melodious stream. But now it was the June of love, and the garden was very fair.

It was nearly luncheon time, and Reggie, in spite of the woodcock, looked on to the cottage, where a thin, blue smoke rose, on a hill above the trees, wondering whether Gertrude had come yet. The beat lay over uneven ground, with some thick cover, interspersed with heathery, open places, on the edges of which many woodcock rose in silent and ghostly flight for the last time. Reggie was an excellent shot, and was having a match with Percy—a shilling a woodcock—which promised to be an investment with good security, and quick returns. He was just arguing a disputed point, in which Percy stoutly upheld that a certain bird, at which they had fired simultaneously, was his own, not Reggie's, and that Reggie ought never to have shot at it, as it did not rise to him, when Gertrude appeared on the scene.

She had seen the party approaching from the cottage, and, as it was cold, she had walked on to meet them.

Percy felt much evil satisfaction at her appearance. The ways of women at shooting parties were known to him. Reggie was looking about in a bush, with the keepers, for a bird he had killed, and Gertrude stopped with him. She fully justified Percy's expectations.

'Oh! Reggie, what a pretty bird. It's an awful shame to shoot them. Poor dear! Oh! I am sure I saw it flap its wings. It can't be dead. Oh! do kill it, quick. I think you're perfectly brutal. Now, you've killed it,' she added with reproach, as if the object of shooting woodcock was to render them immortal.

They soon caught up the others, and Percy's wicked wish was fulfilled. No man in the world can shoot when his affianced is walking by him, making remarks on the weather, and on his home-spun stockings, and telling him that she was sure he didn't hold his gun straight that time. But Reggie did not feel as if he had lost very much, when he handed Percy one-and-ninepence at lunch, which was the nearest equivalent he had for two shillings.

Mrs Davenport was sitting by the fire when they came in, preferring to get warm passively, rather that actively.

'Well, boys,' she said, 'have you had good sport? Fifteen woodcock? How jolly!'

'And we should have got four more if Gertrude hadn't joined us,' said Reggie. 'Why did you let her come, mother?'

Gertrude looked at him in genuine, wide-eyed astonishment.

'What *have* I done, you stupid boy?' she exclaimed. 'I only told you to hold your gun straighter; you were aiming at least five feet from the bird. Besides, it's horrid to kill woodcock; they're such jolly little beasts—birds, I mean.'

'Then why did you tell me to aim straighter?' asked Reggie, with reason.

'Oh, I thought it would please you to kill them, my lord,' she said. 'At least, that's why you went out, wasn't it?'

Reggie was emptying his pockets of cartridges in the porch, and Gertrude was standing in the doorway, so that they were in comparative privacy.

'Would you rather please me than save the woodcock?' he asked softly.

'Reggie, I know those cartridges will go off if you drop them about so. Yes, on the whole, I would. How dirty your hands are. Oh! is that blood on them?'

'No, dear, it's red paint, like what the Indians put on when they go out hunting.'

'You extremely silly boy. Go and wash them, and

then come to lunch. I'll come with you to the little
pump round the corner. You can't be trusted alone.'

'You'll catch cold standing about,' said Reggie,
not without a purpose.

'No more than you will. Besides, I want to
talk to you.'

'Talk away, I'm listening.'

'Oh, well, it's nothing, really. I only meant to
chat.'

'Let's chat, then.'

Well, stoop down, while I pump on your hands.
Do you know, I'm rather happy.'

'What a funny coincidence; so am I.'

And they went back to the house, feeling that
they had had quite a successful conversation. But
that was all they said.

Mr Davenport was to join them after lunch, and
go on shooting with Percy, and they had nearly
finished when he entered. He was a stout, hearty-
looking man of fifty, and inexpressible satisfaction
was his normal expression.

'Well, you people look pretty comfortable,' he
said. 'What sport, Reggie?'

'Oh! rabbits, lots of them, a few hares, ditto

I

pheasants, and fifteen woodcock,' said Reggie, with
his mouth full of bread and cheese, whose naturally
healthy appetite had not been spoiled by love.

'Reggie's going to take Gertrude a drive after
lunch,' said Mrs Davenport ; 'and I shall walk
home ; I want a walk.'

Gertrude and Reggie looked at each other, but
acquiesced.

'Reggie, dear, give Gertrude my furs. She will
be cold driving, and I sha'n't want them walking,'
said Mrs Davenport, as the two started to go.

Reggie took them, and with those little attentions
that a woman loves so much when they are offered
by somebody, wrapped them closely round her.

'Well, I'm sure I ought to be warm enough,'
she said, as they left the door.

'Reggie will take off his coat if you're not, I
daresay,' murmured Mrs Davenport, as she watched
them start. 'Dear boy, how happy he is.'

'He hasn't got much to complain of,' said his
father. 'How old it makes one feel.'

He stretched out his hand to his wife, and she
took it silently. Parents feel old and young when
they see the young birds mate.

'Reggie was recommending me to fall in love as quickly as possible, last night,' remarked Percy. 'He said there was nothing like it.'

Mr Davenport laughed.

'Cheeky young brute,' he said. 'He gives himself the airs of an old married man. He quite patronised his uncle the other day, because he was a bachelor. He and Gertrude together don't make up more than forty-five years between them.'

'Reggie's only just twenty-four,' said Mrs Davenport, 'and she's barely twenty. How dreadfully funny their first attempt at housekeeping will be. Reggie never knows what he's eating, as long as there's plenty of it, and I don't think she does either.'

'Ah! well, shoulder of mutton and love is a very good diet,' said his father. 'Are you ready, Percy? If so, we'll be off.'

Mrs Davenport sat a little longer over the fire before she set out on her homeward walk, and observed, with some annoyance, that it had begun to snow heavily, and half wished she had driven home with Reggie. The keeper's wife wanted to send a boy with her, as the short cut across country, which she meant to take, was hardly more than a sheep - track, running across a flat stretch of bleak moorland.

There is, perhaps, nothing so bewildering as a snow-storm. The thick network of falling flakes conceals all but the nearest objects; and the small, familiar landmarks of the path are soon lost under the white trouble. The consequence was that, half an hour after Mrs Davenport had started, she was entirely at sea as to her position, and, after trying in vain to retrace her steps, she found herself, at the end of an hour's tedious tramp, at a little cottage some six miles from home. She was known to the labourer who lived there, but, as she was too tired to continue walking through the snow that was already beginning to lie somewhat thickly on the path, he sent out a lad to the neighbouring village to procure any sort of conveyance. All this took time, and Mrs Davenport was impatient, for the sake of those at home, to get off as soon as possible. Her husband, she knew, would be very anxious; and there were people coming to dinner.

Meanwhile, Reggie and Gertrude had got safely home after a most satisfactory drive. In fact, they rather liked the snow, which compelled them to go slower, for the sake of that sense of extreme privacy, —a sort of cutting off from the rest of the world—which it lent them. He had said once, 'I am afraid mother will have a horrid walk,' and Gertrude was filled with an evanescent compunction for having taken her furs, but no more allusion was made to it.

They reached home about half-past four, and, half an hour later, were joined by the shooters, who had given up when the snow began in earnest. They were sitting at tea in the dark, oak-panelled hall, by a splendid fire of logs, when Mr Davenport suddenly said,—

'I suppose your mother is changing her things upstairs, Reggie?'

Reggie was sitting on the floor, with his long legs drawn up, and a teacup balanced somewhat precariously on his knees. His back was supported against the head of the sofa, on which Gertrude was sitting. She had put on an amazing tea-gown, of some dark, mazarine stuff, trimmed with large bunches of lace, and was feeling intensely happy and rather languid after the day in the cold air.

She had just asked Reggie some question, and he did not hear, or, at any rate, did not fully take in his father's remark.

Ten minutes passed, and Mr Davenport rose to go.

'You'd better ring the bell, Reggie,' he said, 'and get your mother's maid to take her some tea upstairs, or it will be getting cold. I am afraid she must have got very wet.'

'I don't think mother's come in yet,' said Reggie, placidly.

'Not in yet,' he said quickly. 'Why didn't you tell me? She must have lost her way over the High Croft.'

The irrepressible satisfaction had died out of his face. He rang the bell sharply.

'Tell two men to go at once, with lanterns, over the High Croft. Mrs Davenport must have lost her way.'

Gertrude got up.

'You're not anxious about her, are you?'

'No, no, dear,' said he, 'but it's a horrid night. The snow may be lying very thick, and perhaps she has lost her path. There's no anxiety.'

Gertrude looked down with a little impatience at her long-limbed lover.

'Reggie, you goose, why didn't you remember she hadn't come in?'

Reggie looked up.

'I thought nothing about it. There are lots of cottages about. It was stupid of me to forget. Can I do anything, father? Shall I go out with the men?'

He was perfectly willing to do quite cheerfully all that was required of him, and he would have got back into his damp shooting clothes, and left this comfortable hall and Gertrude without a murmur.

'No, never mind,' said he. 'I think I shall go with them, because I couldn't keep quiet at home. But I wish you'd remembered sooner.'

Reggie had risen and was standing by the fireplace.

'I wish you'd let me go, instead of you,' he said.

'No; there's no need whatever. I only go for my own sake.'

Reggie was quite content. If he was not wanted to go, he was quite happy to stop. He was extremely fond of his mother, and the thought of her possible discomfort was most unpleasant to him, but what was the good of worrying? There was absolutely no danger. Mrs Davenport was an eminently sensible person, and he could not lessen her discomfort by thinking about it. Let us be sensible by all means; let us take things as they come, without thinking about them when there is nothing to be done. Truly these boyish natures are a little irritating at times!

Mr Davenport left the hall and Reggie resumed his place on the floor, and had another cup of tea.

'Poor mother!' he said with sincerity; 'how dreadfully wet and cold she will be.'

Percy had retired to the smoking-room, and the two were alone.'

'Your father was rather vexed,' she said.

'I'm afraid he was,' said Reggie. 'I wish he'd let me go instead of him.'

'Why don't you go with him?'

'That would do no good,' said Reggie. 'He's only going because he is anxious. I'm not the least anxious. Mother is sure to have turned in at some cottage to wait till the snow was over, or until she could get a carriage. If I could save her anything by going out, of course I'd go.'

Gertrude was frowning at the fire.

'I think I'll ask him whether I may come with him,' she said.

Reggie raised his eyebrows.

'Oh, nonsense,' he said. 'He wouldn't let you, anyhow. Sit down, Gerty, and talk.'

'Oh, well,' she said, 'I suppose it's all right.'

There was no need, however, for Mr Davenport to go out, for before he came down again with thick boots, and rough clothes on, his wife had arrived.

Reggie sprang up and welcomed her with great eagerness and affection.

'Dear mother,' he cried, 'I am so glad you have come. Oh! how wet you are.'

He led her to the fire, and poured out a cup of tea with almost feminine tenderness.

'I hope you and Gerty weren't anxious,' she said.

'Oh, no,' said Reggie, frankly, 'not a bit. I knew it would be all right. But I'll run to tell father. He was going out with two men to look for you.'

'Reggie wanted to go instead of him,' said Gertrude, feeling that her lover's conduct was capable of some slight justification.

'Dear Reggie is never anxious,' said Mrs Davenport, warming her hands. 'It is a great comfort for him.'

Gertrude was rather relieved. There was no need for her, apparently, to turn advocate.

CHAPTER II

THEOLOGY, in theory, at any rate, teaches us
that human beings are living things with
souls ; experience, on the other hand, which deals
with facts capable of proof, insists that, whatever
theological truth this statement may embody, for
practical purposes, human beings are born without
souls. The soul awakes, or, as experience says, is
born at varying times. Some men and women reach
maturity of body and mind without it, some, we cannot help thinking, reach death without it ; some, on
the other hand, are but children when that perplex-
ing gift is handed over to their bewildered keeping.
But the soulless human animal often has at its
disposal and use a quantity of instincts which partake of the soul-like nature ; the soul, at any rate,
when it is born, takes them over entire. There is
no need to adapt them, or to purify them, for they

are already clean and pure ; it hardly ever vitalises them, for they are already very living ; it merely shows them their kinship to itself, and they are forthwith embodied in it.

This birth of the soul, like all births, is the consummation of bitter pangs ; it is brought forth in sorrow, through some rending asunder of the inmost fibre, not by any elegant musing on devotional books, nor in a flash of blinding ecstasy, but in silence, save, perhaps, for the bitter cry, in darkness, in solitary desolation, for the sufferer does not know what is happening until the end of his pain has come ; the blind pangs get fiercer and fiercer, and are still unexplained till the light breaks.

It would, perhaps, be an insult to the reader to state baldly the bearing of these remarks, for it will be already, we hope, obvious to him that, in this sense, Reggie, in spite of his frank charm, his susceptibility, his pretty face, his capacity for receiving and inspiring affection, was, at heart, soulless. His strong, hearty liking for his betrothed was of that genial, animal kind, which, however wholesome and satisfactory, has no more to do with the soul than his power of aiming straight at woodcock. Happily,

or unhappily, for him, the abstruse side of life was
scarcely less remote from Gertrude than it was from
himself. She had at present no wish and no power
to give anything but the same genial, hearty liking
that she received, a thorough, wholesome affection
in which the nature of both, as far as they were
aware of their nature, shared to the full. Neither
Reggie nor Gertrude had ever fallen in love with an
idea, which is, perhaps, the most exacting lover that
man or woman ever has, but which, being wholly
abstract, is of an entirely different nature from the
love of two young people who admire and like each
other enormously, mind and body. This abstruser
side of life was a complete puzzle to Reggie. To
take a very small but wholly appropriate illustra-
tion ; he could sympathise with his mother, who might,
perhaps, be wandering on the High Croft in a snow-
storm, with a good deal of feeling, but the instinct
that made his father put on his damp shooting
clothes, and prepare to go out, not for any assist-
ance he could give, but for the eminently unpractical
reason that his wife was in the snow and he was
having tea, seemed inexplicable to his son. If he
could have done a jot or a tittle of good by standing

in the water butt for five minutes, there is not the
shadow of doubt that he would have done so, shiver-
ingly but contentedly and without question ; but it
would have seemed absurd to him to put his nose
outside the hall door, if nothing was to come of it.

With a less sweet disposition, he would have been
a profound egoist ; but in his manliness was salt
enough, as the phrase is, to keep him sweet. The
egoist rates himself higher than he rates the rest of
the world ; he thinks more of himself, consciously or
unconsciously, as he thinks less of others, whereas
Reggie, though he was incapable of those intricacies
of feeling, which, for all practical purposes, are different, not merely in complexity but in kind, from
the simpler forms, and which make the spectacle of
the human race so vastly interesting, and produce,
it may be, love of the complex order, never contem-
plated himself at all, and, however little he knew of
others, at any rate he knew nothing of himself. His
mind resembled, it is true, a being of two dimensions,
which is unable to contemplate the existence of a
third, but in its two dimensions it moved very
smoothly, and had a very charming smile for its
own plane horizon.

Gertrude stopped with the Davenports nearly a
fortnight—a fortnight of pleasant, quiet days, which
are paradise to a mind content, and she was
supremely content. Reggie was all that a lover,
whom she would choose, should be ; he was uniformly
cheerful, affectionate, charming, full of the thought of
her ; and, ah ! how much that means ! Reggie was
one of those who show their best side when they are
in love ; whereas many men, who are otherwise reasonable beings, behave like spoiled children when they
are in that predicament ; they become observant,
jealous, exacting, when they should be serene, in-
dulgent, large-hearted.

But once, just at the end of that fortnight, there
arose out of the sea a little cloud like a man's hand,
which broke the blue horizon, though Reggie was
unconscious of it. A little hint of it had occurred
once before, on that evening when Mrs Davenport
lost her way over the High Croft, but on that
occasion it had soon passed away.

Percy, it must be owned, was not so jovially con-
tented with the spectacle, as the days went on, as
the actors themselves. He was a deductive young
gentleman, and, to his mind, this affair resembled too

strongly Reggie's previous flutterings in the feminine
dovecotes to strike him as something altogether
different from a flirtation on a large scale. A
flirtation, after all, is only a superficial exhibition of
love, an attraction on one side, a liability to be
attracted on the other ; and the question occurred to
him, whether it is possible to keep a flirtation up
permanently, and what was left if it broke down?
A strong, deep love, like the Nile in flood, leaves, like
a sediment behind, which in so many cases renders
marriages, from which the tumultuous stream has
passed, happy and stable, an alluvial deposit, which
makes the earth rich and fruitful in the sober green
of friendship ; but when the slender, light-hearted
streamlet is dried up, the effect of its passage is only
too often seen in the uncovering of ugly roots and
stones, and a removal, not a deposit of sediment.
Of course he knew more about those previous affairs,
which, to do Reggie justice, were superficial and
innocent enough, than did that gentleman's mother.
A young man, whatever his relations with his mother
may be, will choose some other confidant in such
cases.   They argued, in fact, nothing more than a
very great susceptibility on Reggie's part to the

influence of charming young women, and the sage
Percy asked himself whether the constant propin-
quity of one specimen of this attractive product
would necessarily secure him from the influence of
the others. That unlucky resemblance between his
previous skirmishes and this engagement seemed
to him too close to be altogether satisfactory. A
flirtation on a large scale, he argued, is not very
different from a flirtation on a small scale.

Mrs Davenport had immense confidence in Percy.
He was three years older than Reggie, and was
possessed of a certain soundness, of which that
young gentleman stood in need. He had been of
great use to him in the thousand and one unconscious ways in which one young man can help
another slightly younger than himself. He had
a practical mastery of details that led him to re-
liable conclusions on their sum, which is a gift as
useful as intuitive judgment, though less striking
in its process, as it partakes of the nature of industry rather than brilliance. But Reggie's mother
did him justice, and found herself consulting him
as she would have consulted an older man, with
considerable respect for his opinion.

K

'We are all so delighted about Reggie's engagement,' she said to him one evening after dinner.
'His father thought, and so did I, that a long
engagement was better. You see they are both
very young, and they ought to know each other
well. No one should marry on an enthusiastic first
impression, least of all Reggie, because he has so
many of them.'

'Certainly there are no signs of wavering yet,'
said he. 'They are as fond of each other as—
as two children.'

'Why do you say that?' she asked.

'They are so healthily fond of each other,' he
said. 'They were trying to read two of Browning's
lyrics this morning, about one way of love and
another way of love, and they gave it up in about
three minutes and read Pickwick instead.'

'Poor Reggie, I'm afraid he'll find that his way
of love is neither one nor the other, but I think
it's a good way for all that.'

'There's no nonsense about it, anyhow,' said
Percy, without meaning to make reflections on
the lyrics in question.

'It isn't tumultuous exactly,' said Reggie's mother,

'but it's very thorough. Still waters do run deep, you know, in spite of the proverb.'

'But the stillness is not a proof of their depth.'

'No; but when a stream is in the rapids, so to speak, it is. The rapids, I mean, which come just after the waterfall, the plunge into love.'

'Oh, but Reggie's always falling in love.'

'So I gathered; though, of course, the boy wouldn't tell me about that. But I don't think that's against his present engagement.'

Percy was silent, and Mrs Davenport adjusted her bracelet before she added,—

'I believe it's a healthy thing for a young man to be in a chronic state of devotion. The vague adoration is all sucked into the particular adoration when that comes.'

'But is falling in love with a series of particular girls to be called a vague adoration?'

'Yes, certainly, just as a circle is an infinite number of straight lines. He falls in love with womanliness in many forms.'

'I see. No doubt you are right. Certainly he is standing his long engagement very well.'

'Poor boy! he wants to shorten it very much,

which is just the very reason why I want it to be long.'

'Miss Carston is satisfied, I gather?'

'It looks like it,' said Mrs Davenport, smiling, and indicating with her eye a shady corner of the room where the two lovers were sitting.

'Old Lady Hayes was staying with us for a week in London last summer,' she continued, after a pause. 'She was defeated in a great battle, apparently, with your sister, and came here to bind up her wounds by bullying us all. I have an immense admiration for anyone who can rout her.'

Percy laughed.

'I heard something about it. Eva behaved abominably, I expect.'

'I met her several times in London,' said Mrs Davenport. 'She has a wonderful way of appearing to notice no one, and obliging every one to notice her.'

'I never saw anyone so changed in a short time as Eva,' said Percy. 'She has suddenly found men and women extraordinarily interesting. A year ago, she was exactly the reverse. She disliked most women, and never remembered any man.'

'That was the impression she gave me in the summer.'

'Ah! but that manner is only a survival. She is often silent; at other times she talks a great deal. In the old days she seldom talked at all.'

'Poor Hayes is terribly afraid of her.'

'I think most people are afraid of her. She can be very cruel.'

'A woman with such beauty as that has an unfair advantage. Her shots must always tell.'

'She is one of those people who always make an impression,' said Percy; 'because she doesn't care at all what impression she makes.'

'That is the sort of impression that produces the deadliest results,' said Mrs Davenport. 'If a man sees that he is being made a fool of, he can be on his guard, but the effect of the other is that he is dazzled, piqued, maddened. The women who don't care are always those for whom men care most passionately.'

'I wonder if Eva will ever fall in love,' said Percy half to himself.

'It will be a fine sight if she does; she will teach all these bloodless people how to do it. I think she has more force than anyone I know. Does she ever talk to you about her marriage?'

'Oh! there's nothing in the world she doesn't talk about. She has begun to take an immense interest in herself, as well as in other people, and she watches her own development with much entertainment. She never forces anything; she quietly waits till the change is made, and then finds out exactly what has happened.'

'Her scene with old Lady Hayes must have been wicked,' said Mrs Davenport. 'I can imagine her so well, lolling back in her chair with infinite languor, smoking cigarettes probably, and uttering slow, polished blasphemies about all her mother-in-law's most cherished beliefs.'

'They are out in Algiers now,' said Percy. 'Eva suddenly expressed a wish to go there again. She likes the languid heat of the place. Jim Armine is with them.'

Ah!' said Mrs Davenport, softly. 'She is very cruel.'

'She had the greatest distaste for her ordinary home life. Last year my father lost a lot of money, and we had to live very quietly at home

in the country and retrench.   Eva couldn't endure it.
She had quite made up her mind that she would
never fall in love at all.   She will do something
sublime if she does.   She is quite capable of sacri-
ficing herself or anybody else.'

'A clear stage and a crowd to see,' thought Mrs
Davenport, 'and may I be in the stalls.'

Meanwhile, the two lovers were talking at the very
farthest corner of the drawing-room, but before the
evening was over, the little cloud, which had just
appeared over the horizon on the occasion when
Reggie's mother had lost her way in the snow,
gathered again, and this time it seemed to Gertrude
to leave a little film of mist behind.   Like the other
two, they had been talking about Percy's sister, and
Reggie had said suddenly,—

'She is perfectly lovely, I believe ; they call her
the most beautiful woman in London.   Percy showed
me her photograph.   I want to see her very much.'

This speech, made in absolute thoughtlessness,
jarred somehow on Gertrude's sensibilities.

'I daresay there are many actresses as beautiful,'
she said, rather unnecessarily.   'I don't think I
should like her a bit.   There was a man staying

with us the other day who said she was perfectly
reckless about what she did.'

'Oh! a woman as beautiful as that can afford to
be reckless,' said Reggie. 'She sets the fashion.'

'I don't think recklessness is a good fashion to
set, then,' said Gertrude, with some asperity.

'Oh! nor do I,' said Reggie. 'I only meant that
one excuses it more, somehow.'

'I don't see why you should excuse it because a
woman is beautiful,' said she, seeing the cloud rising
out of the sea.

'I don't know,' said Reggie. 'You must take a
person all round; beauty is an advantage, and you
set it off against a corresponding disadvantage.'

'Do you mean that an incomparably beautiful
woman is excusable if she does unpardonably nasty
things?'

'I suppose it comes to that in extremities,' said
he, doubtfully. 'You see, it is impossible to believe
that such a woman could do anything quite un-
pardonable.'

'Reggie, you're absurd,' she cried; 'don't talk such
utter nonsense, and be thankful I don't believe you
mean what you say.'

Reggie turned round in surprise.

'Why, Gerty, what's the matter?' he asked.

'You hurt me when you talk like that,' she said.

'Oh! what have I been saying?' said he, with an air of perplexity. 'You know the worst of me is, I never know what I'm talking about. When I begin talking I get dreadfully puzzled.'

'Most people explain what they mean by talking, not obscure it.'

'Well, it's just the opposite way with me,' said he serenely. 'I know what I think all right before I begin to say it, but as soon as I begin to say it, I begin not to know what I think.'

This confident assertion failed to satisfy Gertrude.

'You said you didn't mind a woman being immoral, if she was only beautiful,' she said.

'Oh! I never said a word about immorality,' exclaimed Reggie. 'I don't think it's right to talk about such things. Gerty, what *do* you mean? As if I should say such things to you, especially since I never think them at all.'

The open candour of her lover's face had its due effect.

'Well, you're quite sure you meant nothing of the sort, are you?' she asked, ready to be mollified.

'Of course I am,' said he with sincerity. 'I don't understand what you mean.'

'What did you say, then?'

The cloud had begun to drift, but the horizon was not clear yet.

'Oh! don't ask me,' he said tragically. 'I tell you I never know what I say, and I get so dreadfully confused. I said—Oh, Lord! what did I say? I said that an ugly woman—oh, dear!—that an ugly woman can't do the things which, if a beautiful woman did, she wouldn't be thought a beast,' he explained, with a fine disregard of coherency.

'Oh! but, Reggie, that's exactly what you said you didn't say.'

'No, it isn't,' said Reggie, who, though not exactly bored, wanted to talk about something else. 'I said something about a beautiful woman being the fashion, which an ugly woman can't be.'

'What do you mean by the fashion?'

'Why, I mean the fashion,' said Reggie; 'the rage, the *comme il* something, the thing everybody else does—balloon sleeves and dachshunds, you know.'

'Are you sure you only meant that sort of
fashion?' asked she.

'Oh! yes, of course I am. Oh! do let's talk about
something else.'

But Gertrude was vaguely dissatisfied. The cloud
had left a little drift of mist behind.

And Reggie? Well, Reggie's cleanly, honest
instincts gave him no directions on this subject;
they drew in their feelers like sea anemones when
a foreign substance touches them. A soul would
have had a word or two to say to him about it, but
Reggie unfortunately knew nothing about that.

They sat silent for a minute or two, Reggie trying
to think of something to say which should be
sufficiently remote from this puzzling topic, Gertrude
still rather troubled in her mind. In after years,
she remembered that night as the first occasion on
which a certain vague pain had begun, the first of
a series of blind pangs that stirred a new sort of
feeling in her, that tore asunder some fibre in her
inmost being. An elegant musing over devotional
books is, as I have mentioned before, the accredited
source of such an awakening.

The unerring instinct of a lover in Reggie, divined,

though very dimly, that some little change had taken place. He felt that Gertrude had felt something that he had not felt. In spite of his recent sense of irresponsibility, of utter contentedness on his own part, he could see that the edge had been taken, ever so slightly, off hers. You may observe something like this in the case of the more human animals. A dog sometimes will know that it does not understand, if the bond between itself and its human friend is very strong. Its inability to understand is something quite different; it is the knowledge of this inability that is rare, and Reggie felt this now.

As is natural, he recovered himself first. After a twinge of pain, one is prone to sit quiet a minute or two, and regain one's normal level. But the pain had been all on one side, and Gertrude required a little space to steady herself in.

'Gerty, let's play a game of some sort. Come and see what the others are going to do.'

He got up and stood in front of her.

'Pull me up,' she said.

Her white hands lay in his great, brown paws, like little patches of snow in some sheltered nook of the hills. But they were warm with life and love, and she was very fair. He bent down and kissed them gently, first one and then the other.

'You sha'n't kiss my hands,' she said. 'Come, let's go to the others.'

The troubled look had gone from her face, but Mrs Davenport, with a woman's swift, infallible intuition, saw that something, ever so small, had happened. There was still in her eyes the shadow of a vague wonder.

Ladies, I believe, have a bad habit of going to each other's bedrooms when they are thought to have gone to bed, and sitting by the fire, talking things over. It is a bad plan to talk things over at night, because, while you are talking, there forms in the air, without your seeing it, a little grey ghost, to which your words give birth. There are no such things as barren words; all words uttered by you go to make up a little series of figures, who come and talk to you when nobody else is there. And the sort of conversation that Gertrude and Mrs Davenport had that night gave rise to a little, pale, anxious, grey ghost, that sat by Gertrude's bedside, and, as soon as her body had

had enough sleep—the ghost always allows his victims the necessary minimum—it tapped fretfully on her shoulder, and said, 'Come, wake up, let us go on talking!' And Gertrude stirred in her dreamless sleep, and knew that the little ghost had come to talk to her.

It is a time-honoured custom for an author to describe the personal appearance of any character when he decides to lay his reflections before a discriminating public, and the neglect of this custom is a red rag to the stupid, furious bull called criticism So, since this little ghost's personal appearance is only to be described by retailing the conversation which took place between Gertrude and Mrs Davenport the night before, this obedient and peace-loving author complies with the eminently English demand.

Gertrude was sitting before her fire in her dressing-gown, when Mrs Davenport came in. Her eyes still wore a troubled look, and the pictures in the fire were not so pleasant as she had known them.

Mrs Davenport noticed it at once. It was the same look as she had seen before that evening, a little intensified.

'Are you tired, dear?' she asked. 'Would you rather I left you to go to bed instead of talking?'

Gertrude looked up.

'No, I want to talk very much.'

'Gerty, dear, is anything the matter?'

'I don't know.'

There was a short silence. Mrs Davenport was far too wise to press her. Then Gertrude said,—

'Do you know Lady Hayes?'

Mrs Davenport was puzzled. The carrier-pigeon always takes a few wide circles before he sets out on his unerring flight home.

'Oh! yes, quite well,' she replied. 'Percy and I were talking about her this evening. It's funny that neither you nor Reggie have even seen her.'

She was feeling her way with tactful discretion. But it was a very narrow path down which Gertrude meant to go, and Mrs Davenport not unnaturally had missed it.

'What is she like?' asked Gertrude.

'Ah! what isn't she like? She is the most beautiful woman in England, I think, also one of the most reckless, and, I believe, very generous. I should call her dangerous as well. But she is so interesting, so unlike others, that you forget everything else, which is harder than forgiving it.'

Gertrude turned round and faced her.

'Ah! you too,' she said.

'I don't quite understand, dear,' said Mrs Davenport, gently; 'have you and Reggie been talking about her? Tell me, Gerty. I saw something was a wee bit wrong. I'm sure you haven't been quarrelling, though. What has been the matter?'

'I couldn't love Reggie more than I do,' said Gertrude, irrelevantly, 'and I don't think he could love me more than he does. It's odd that I should be troubled.'

'Yes, dear, I am sure of your love for each other,' said Mrs Davenport. 'But tell me what is wrong. It does one good to tell things; they become so much smaller in the telling. Those vague thoughts are like those great spongy puff balls that we noticed to-day; as soon as you really examine them, you find there is nothing in them. What is it?'

'I don't know,' said Gertrude again.

Ah, that infinite patience of womankind! Mrs Davenport waited a moment, and then, by an unerring instinct, laid her hand softly on Gertrude's, and pressed it gently. The touch had power in it, and the dumb soul spake.

'I've got no right to be troubled,' said Gertrude, 'and I feel it's horribly ungrateful of me, when I think of what Reggie is to me, and how good you are all to me. But—'

Her voice got tremulous, and she stopped abruptly.

'Yes?' said Mrs Davenport, softly, wanting to hear more for Gertrude's sake.

'It's just this,' she said at last, speaking rapidly, and with a splendid self-control. 'Reggie said something this evening which hurt me. He said that recklessness mattered less in a beautiful woman than in another.'

'Is that all?' said Mrs Davenport, with considerable relief.

'No, that's not all,' said Gertrude. 'That was all nonsense; of course I know he doesn't mean that. But he didn't see it hurt me. Oh! it's so hard not to give you a wrong impression. I don't mean that he was inconsiderate at all—he never is anything but considerate—but he simply didn't know. It wasn't tangible to his mind. If I cut my finger he'd be miserable about it, but somehow he was unable to understand how this hurt me, and

L.

so he could not see that it did hurt me. It hurt me somewhere deep down, ever so little, but the feeling was new and strange. This sounds horribly selfish, I'm afraid, but I can't help it.'

'Ah, I think I see,' said Mrs Davenport.

'It's like this,' said Gertrude. 'Hitherto I've always felt so entirely at one with Reggie. If I feel a thing, he's always seemed to feel it too, like an echo, and the same with me. But just this once I listened for the echo and it didn't come.'

Mrs Davenport paused a moment.

'Did you ever hear of the man who was out riding with his wife when her horse threw her, and in dismounting to help her he dropped his whip, and while he was picking it up, the horse kicked her and killed her?' she asked. 'It seems to me that you are just a little like that man, Gerty. Love is a very big thing; one's own small sensibilities are very little things. Take care of the big thing, never mind the others.'

'But they're so mixed up,' said the girl. 'You see the little thing is a part of the big thing.'

'You are right—that is quite true. But there are many very lovely things which it is right to look at as a whole. Love is one of those. All philosophers, from the beginning of the world, have addled their brains over that impossible analysis. You and Reggie are not philosophers, Gerty; you are young lovers, and it is not your business to analyse or dissect, but to enjoy.'

Mrs Davenport was at the sore disadvantage of having to temporise. She could not but suspect what was at the bottom of this. But all she said was quite sincere. She fully believed that the strength of Gerty's love would fill the interval, if there was to be an interval between her and Reggie. It is best that the woman be better, finer, bigger than the man, for the beautiful indulgence of a woman's love has more passive endurance in these early stages than a man's. In the perfect marriage, the two eventually are mixed 'in spite of the mortal screen,' but such mixings are rare at first. They rushed together, they will inevitably recoil a little, and a woman has more power of waiting for that final joining together again than most men. Gertrude seemed somewhat relieved, but it was not quite over yet. The grey ghost was waiting for his frillings.

' I was just a little disappointed, you understand ? ' she said. ' I waited for the echo, but it never came. Ah ! well, I am very happy. You are very good to me.'

' God forbid that I or mine should ever give you pain, said Mrs Davenport, warmly.

' And what am I to do ? ' said Gertrude, to whom the practical side of things always presented itself.

' Be natural, dear,' said the other, ' as you always are. You are both very young ; well, that is a gift almost more worth having than anything else. It lies in your power a great deal to keep it. And, if you guard it well, it will build up in you the only other gift which is worth having, which will last you to your grave. They will melt into each other.'

Gertrude looked at her inquiringly.

' It is called by many names,' she said. ' It is trustfulness, it is serenity, it is sympathy ; it is all these, and many more. Some people call it the grace of God, and I think they are right.' She kissed the girl on her forehead very tenderly. ' It will tide you over the difficult places, over which youth carries you now, for youth has the gift of a splendid stainlessness—of going through deep waters and not being drowned, of avoiding evil instinctively,

without thought; but the time comes to us all when
we avoid it with our reason as well, and with our soul.'

'It was ridiculous of me,' said the girl suddenly.
'Reggie didn't know what I felt, and I didn't tell
him; and yet I was disappointed. I've probably
done just the same to him lots of times, and he
never told me. It was abominably selfish of me.
I hope he'll forgive me.'

'I should think it extremely unlikely,' said Mrs
Davenport, with enormous gravity. 'I should ad-
vise you to cry yourself to sleep. I am going to
bed, and so are you. Good-night! Ah! my dear,
I pray you may be very happy.'

Gertrude clung to her in a long kiss, feeling a
new bond had sprung up between them.

But the odious, little, grey ghost, who had been
grinning sardonically at her easy enthusiasm, was
sitting by her bed, waiting till the renewal of strength,
brought by sleep, had quickened her capabilities for
listening to his cold accuracies—until that generous,
sudden glow had begun to burn somewhat less
warmly in her breast.

CHAPTER III

L ORD HAYES had been rather troubled about his health during the winter in which the foregoing events had occurred, though it had not stood in the way of their giving several large house-parties. But at one of these he had suddenly fainted dead off in the middle of dinner, and, when the house was empty again, he had gone up to London to see a doctor.

Eva was sitting in her room when he returned, feeling rather bored.

'Well, Hayes,' she said, as he came in, 'what did they say to you?'

Lord Hayes adjusted his trousers about the knee before he answered.

'I have all the symptoms of dangerous heart disease,' he said. 'I may live for many years, and die of something else. Again, I may die almost at any moment.'

Eva's book dropped off her knee.

'How horrible!' she said at length. 'Can nothing be done? Are they sure they are right?'

'Unfortunately, they are quite sure,' he said; 'and nothing can be done. They consider the chance of my dying quite suddenly at any time as possible, but not at all likely.'

Eva, in her serene health, felt a sudden, great pity for him, but not unmixed with horror. She had no sympathy with disease; it seemed to her hardly decent.

'Poor Hayes,' she said. 'I cannot tell you how shocked I am.'

'I thought it was best to tell you,' said he, 'but let us avoid the subject altogether. I shall live to bore you for many years yet.'

Eva looked at him admiringly.

'You are a brave man. But you are right. Don't let us talk about it.'

This took place late in November, but the fact that the symptoms, which had been the result of over-fatigue, did not re-occur, made Eva soon get used to the thought, and, in a measure, her husband too. He took the doctor's advice, did not over-exert himself at all, and found that the discovery they had made did not affect his health. The days soon began to pass on as usual.

Eva had suddenly determined to go abroad for a few weeks, for she had an intense dislike to an English winter. Hence it came about that one morning at breakfast, when she and her husband were alone, she had said to him,—

'What do you propose to do during these next two months, Hayes?'

Lord Hayes looked up from his breakfast, not quite understanding the purport of her question.

'I suppose we shall remain here till Easter,' he said. 'We are paying some visits in January, I believe.'

'I should rather like to go abroad for a few weeks now this horrible weather has begun.' She looked out of the window, where snow was beginning to fall heavily, and shivered sympathetically. 'I hate this English weather,' she said; 'it is like being in a cold bath. Dry cold is not so bad,

there is something exhilarating about it. But this
doesn't suit me in the least. Why shouldn't we
go to Algiers again?'

'I thought you didn't like Algiers,' he said. 'Do
you propose that we should go alone?'

'Oh no, we won't make any intolerable demands
of that sort on each other. I think it suits us best
to have people with us. I daresay Percy would
like to come for a bit, perhaps your mother would
join us, and then there's Jim Armine, who always
wants to go abroad whenever he can.'

Eva spoke with the utmost indifference, but her
husband found himself wondering whether that indifference was not a very subtle piece of acting.
That he had some inkling of the young man's
feelings towards his wife was very possible, but he
had not the least objection to that. In fact, it
rather pleased him than otherwise, as it afforded a
sort of testimonial to his own admirable taste in
wishing her to become his wife, and to his enviable
success in securing her for that purpose. He knew
quite well that the *rôle* of jealous husband would
not suit him in the least, and he had no intention
of being a complaisant one, but he had sense

enough to guess that complaisance was not necessary. He had no reason to believe that Eva had
a heart at all; and he had no desire to make a
mistake. If he suggested to Eva that he would
rather not have Jim Armine with them, his remark
would be liable to be interpreted in a way which
she might with justice resent; in fact, that was the
only intrepretation open to her, for he liked the
young man well enough in himself. He did not
even admit the smallest suspicion into his mind;
he only realised that there was the possibility of
an avenue, down which suspicion might some day
choose to walk; and when suspicion was seen by
him walking down that avenue, he would go and
take its hand, and they would knock at Eva's door,
and show themselves.

Eva rose from the table.

'Then you don't mind coming to Algiers?'

It was clearly impossible to say 'No; but I do
mind Jim Armine coming,' and so he proposed a
date some ten days off for their departure.

'Why shouldn't we go sooner?' asked Eva.

'There's been some unpleasantness down at the
ironworks,' he said, 'and I think that, as owner, I

ought to just wait till it's settled in some form or another.'

'Do you mean down at Trelso?'

'Yes; the men are striking, or wanting to strike, for higher wages—more pay, in fact.'

'Couldn't you go down there to-day, and see the agents or managers or whoever they are?'

'There is nothing definite yet; we only know that there is a good deal of discontent.'

'Surely, then, you can leave it with your manager to deal with, when it occurs. It is absurd waiting in England for a handful of miners to tell you what they want.'

'It would be better, I think, if I waited,' he said.

'I wish you would explain to me exactly why.'

'Simply because, as owner,' he said, 'they would wish to consult me if anything went really wrong.'

'Surely there is a telegraph to Algiers. I should infinitely prefer starting in less than a week. I really cannot stand this sort of weather.'

'I feel sure I am right to stop,' he said. 'It is certainly best.'

Eva hesitated a moment.

'Would you mind my going on without you, then? Perhaps that would be the best plan. I daresay Jim will come with me.'

Her husband looked at her narrowly. He felt he was playing a losing·game.

'I will go down to Trelso to-day, and see exactly what the state of affairs is—how they stand, in fact.'

'Very good. I shall start on Thursday, then. I will write to Jim to-day. I hope you won't lose any more money over this.'

He smiled rather grimly.

'I hope not. This last year has been very expensive. I don't grudge it in the least; in fact, it is very interesting to me to see how much a woman can spend.'

He was conscious of an impotent desire to make it not quite pleasant for Eva, even if she did get her own way in the main, and he was pleased to see her flinch, just perceptibly. She was annoyed with herself for doing it.

'Yes, I suppose you find you spend much more now than you used.'

'About ten thousand a year more.'

'Dear me, that is a great deal. You can hardly have counted the cost.'

'I did not quite realise it at the time. That's what I mean by saying it was more than I anticipated.'

'Ah! of course you wouldn't anticipate it,' said Eva. 'Love is blind, you know.'

Lord Hayes was rather sorry he had begun. He was somewhat in the position of a dog which runs out from its shelter to bite a passer-by, and when it gets into the open, discovers that its intended victim carries a stick.

Eva waited long enough to give him time to reply if he wanted, but finding he said nothing, turned and left the room.

Two days after this, as they were sitting at dinner, Eva asked him what had happened about the ironworks.

'I am glad you reminded me,' he said. 'I told them that I wished particularly to leave England at once, and asked them to telegraph to me in case I was wanted. It appears that they do not expect any immediate disturbance, so I shall be able to come with you on Thursday—in fact, there will be nothing to detain me.'

'You had better stop if you think you are wanted,' said Eva. 'I can manage perfectly by myself, and Jim Armine will be with me; he wrote to-day. But if they don't want you, of course you'll go with me.'

'Armine is coming, then, is he?' asked her husband.

'Yes; you don't object to him, I hope?'

'Not in the least.'

'If you do, it would have been better if you had said so at once,' said Eva, carelessly. 'I've asked him now.'

'Why should you suppose I object to him?' he asked suddenly.

'You didn't seem very cordial about it. Have you asked anybody else?'

'I mentioned it to my mother when I saw her in Trelso, but she said she wouldn't come.'

'Ah!' said Eva, with the ghost of a smile, 'did she say why?'

'Apparently it was for your sake—because of you, in fact.'

'I expect she meant for her own sake. I should be charmed to have her. There is a straightforwardness, a refusal to compromise, in her behaviour to me, that is very refreshing.'

'She speaks of you with bitterness—I might almost say rancour,' remarked Lord Hayes.

'I am more sinned against than sinning, then,' said Eva. 'I always feel perfectly charitable towards her. She loathes me; but, after all, that is not her fault. Really, it is wonderful what a fine order of hatred is compatible with the most orthodox Christianity. But of course I am one of the works of the devil, which she has been led to renounce from a child.'

Thus it came about that, before the middle of December, Lord Hayes and his wife, and Jim Armine, were installed in the charming little villa at Algiers. The Gulf of Lyons was kinder on this occasion to the susceptibilities of Lord Hayes, and he produced his white umbrella, and sat on a deck chair in untroubled contemplation. He always wore a yachtsman's cap and brown shoes on calm trips, which were, somehow, particularly aggravating to Eva.

She was sitting on deck when he came upstairs on the morning after their departure from Marseilles, and Eva had a long, malignant look at him as he approached her.

'You look completely nautical this morning,' she said slowly. 'I hope it won't get rough, for your sake, or you will have to retire. The commodore will be found groaning in his cabin. But, perhaps you are only a fighting sailor, like Lord Nelson, who was always ill, wasn't he? In that case, I hope we sha'n't meet any Moorish privateers. If we are attacked during a storm, you will be completely exposed.'

Eva had rarely said anything to him in such simple bad taste, and her husband was surprised. The childishness of her strictures, however, rather amused him than otherwise, for he thought he had the key to them, in a rather awkward little scene which had taken place the evening before. Eva had been arguing some point with Jim Armine, and he had got a little excited. She had just made an assertion which seemed to him to contradict what she had said a moment before, and by an unlucky slip he exclaimed,—

'Why, Eva, you said just the opposite a minute ago.'

The mistake was pardonable enough : when a man is in love with a woman, he naturally thinks of her by her Christian name, and it is excusable if, in some momentary excitement, he uses it. Eva was startled. He had never called her that before, and, losing her self-control for one half second, she uttered a sudden exclamation of anger, and glanced at her husband. He was sitting with one leg crossed over the other, looking at the sunset. He turned to Jim Armine, and said politely,—

'I think you must have misunderstood Lady Hayes.'

The poor young man flushed deeply, and Eva bit her lips, divided between her annoyance and a desire to laugh. But the annoyance conquered in the end, as the delicate, veiled insult of her husband's speech dawned upon her. His words certainly bore another interpretation, though whether he had meant it or not she was not quite sure, and she could not ask him. But Jim Armine evidently took them in the obscurer sense and was horribly disconcerted, and Eva not unnaturally felt extremely annoyed. He was, possibly, trying to make a fool of her, and she had not the least intention of being treated in such

M

a manner. After a few moments she found something to say, but the conversation was evidently over.
Jim Armine soon strolled away to the other end of
the deck, and Eva was left alone with her husband.

As soon as the other was out of hearing, she said
to him,—

'I do not wish you to speak of me in that way.
Please remember that.'

'I regret having offended you,' replied he, 'but
I do not choose that Armine should call you by
your Christian name, Eva, in fact.'

'Your speech implied more than that,' she said.

Lord Hayes determined to make a stand.

'You are very quick at finding meanings.'

'What you said was insulting.'

'It is insulting to you that he should call you
Eva?'

'Do you admit, then, that your speech bore
another meaning?'

Lord Hayes lit another cigarette.

'I admit nothing of the sort. Not at all.'

'You will be so good as to apologise to him.'

'I have no reason for supposing that he imagined
it to bear any meaning but the obvious one—the one;

in fact, which I meant to convey. Of course you are at liberty to explain to him that, if you choose.'

For the first time Eva was conscious of a slight disadvantage, and Lord Hayes distinctly saw it. As she sat still silent, he looked at his watch and remarked,—

'I am afraid they propose to give us dinner at seven. It is a barbarous custom. Perhaps you would like to know that it is now five minutes to seven.'

He carefully furled his white umbrella, and walked down the deck to the saloon. He made in his mind a careful little note of the occurrence, against that possible contingency of suspicion coming down the avenue. It was characteristic of him that he was as evenly polite as ever to Jim Armine, and advised him to drink white wine and not red, and remarked to him at tea afterwards that the Albert biscuits were stale, but that it was interesting to observe that the English manufactories of biscuits held their own abroad ; in fact, that the makers of the stale Albert biscuits were Huntly & Palmer.

This suggestive little scene accounted, in his mind, for Eva's unusual want of politeness on the subject of his yachtsman's cap and brown canvas shoes.

But he did not consider that a reason for abandoning them; in fact, they became to him a sort of commemorative medal on the occasion of his victory. A force which has an unbroken record of defeat is apt to dwell on a single and unexpected victory. In the main he was right in attributing Eva's irritation that morning to her slight discomfiture on the evening before, for though she had dismissed, or rather forgotten, the occurrence, there was still in her a latent resentment that unconsciously vented itself in this manner.

They had been at the villa four or five days, and Lord Hayes had got into the habit of observing his wife and Jim Armine somewhat closely. Eva was rather silent; to her husband she hardly spoke at all, though now and then at meals she would begin talking, more to herself than the others. Jim Armine was not a very wise young man, and he said things sometimes that, with another woman, would have betrayed him, but Eva did not seem to notice them.

They were seated at lunch one day, when Eva took up her parable. She had said nothing at all, as her way was, for some minutes, and Lord Hayes had been describing to Jim how the eucalpytus oil was extracted from the tree.

'You must excuse my silence, Mr Armine,' she said, 'but, you know, I have all sorts of recollections about this villa. We were here, you know, on our wedding tour, after we had been on the Riviera— just Hayes and myself—and we used to sit out in the garden and listen to the nightingales singing of love. It was very romantic; no doubt Hayes has spoken to you of it, when you pour out your hearts in the smoking-room, after I have gone to bed. It is always odd to me that men choose that time for being confidential. I should have thought it would have disturbed your night's rest.'

'How do you know that we are confidential, then?' asked Jim.

'Why, of course you are; there isn't time to be confidential during the day. Besides, that is the only time when you are sure not to be invaded by women. I shall hide in the smoking-room some night and listen to what you say.'

'There is nothing you might not hear,' said her husband.

'You mean that, I suppose, in order to deter me

from listening, assuming that, being a woman, I only
care to hear what is not meant for my ears. But
you said it very politely.'

'Not at all; it was a formal invitation,' said he,
'an assurance of how entirely welcome you would be.'

'Thanks. Of course you and I are under a sort
of mutual compact to delight in each other's society
at any time or place.'

Lord Hayes laughed.

'One eternal honeymoon. Surely the golden age
will return.'

Jim Armine, not unnaturally, felt that this was
distinctly a comedy *à deux*, and that the presence
of a third person was unnecessary. But no man can
leave his red mullet half eaten for such reasons.
Everything goes to the wall before our material needs.

Lord Hayes's punctilious little manner always van-
ished in anything like a scene. He began to be self-
possessed at exactly that point when most self-pos-
sessed people begin to be nervous and flurried, for his
punctiliousness was the result not of nervousness, but
a desire not to be nervous, and when the occasion
was interesting enough to allow him to forget this,
his tinge of finished cynicism and indifference to his

fellow men assumed its natural predominance. He
rather enjoyed a little polite sparring match with his
wife, until he began to get the worst of it; as long as
the buttons were on the foils he could fence very
decently, but the sight of the bare point distinctly
discomposed him.

Eva flushed.

'Let us reserve our raptures for when we are
alone,' she said. 'They are slightly embarrassing to
a third person.'

Lord Hayes smiled. For the second time the
banner of victory seemed to wave over his head.
He saw his wife flush, and knew that she was very
angry. That desire to avenge herself which she had
felt so strongly on her return from her honeymoon,
the sense that she had been trapped, and was being
exhibited as a rare bird in a cage, was very strong in
her; the added insolence of the trapper pretending
to be on intimate and loving terms with her made
her furious, and the consciousness that she had
brought it upon herself, did not tend to diminish
her rage. For the second time he was trying to
make a fool of her before a third person.

How far a scene that took place a day or two

after this was brought on by Eva's dislike of her husband and her thirst for vengeance, is not part of this narrative to determine. The chronicler's mission is not to form conclusions, but to present data, and my immediate mission is to present some rather important data.

Even in December, in Algiers, it is often pleasant to sit out of doors at nine in the evening, for the air is cool but dry, and Eva often spent an hour in the little open passage which ran round the central courtyard of the house, and in which, a year before, she had talked to her husband on the position of women. This time it was Jim Armine who was her companion; Lord Hayes had gone upstairs to write to his mother, and he proposed to give her some accurate descriptions, based on observation, about the date palm.

His room looked out on to the afore-mentioned courtyard, and before beginning his letter, he went across to the window to close it, for he had heard that the night air of Algiers is unwholesome. Just as he was in the act of taking this little pre-caution, there lighted on his ear the grumbling noise of a basket-chair being dragged in passive, grating resistance over a stone floor, followed by the sound of Eva's voice. As he could not see her, he came to the very logical conclusion that she was sitting directly below his window, and where she could not see him, and as she was talking, and Jim Armine was the only person in the house, he pictured her talking to him. After all, the evening air was not unpleasant, and instead of closing the window he stood by it and listened. The emphatic deliberation of this manœuvre was, he felt vaguely, in its favour from a conventional point of view.

The voices, at first, were inaudible to him, for the sense of hearing requires focussing as much as the sense of sight, and he only caught a word here and there. But, for the sake of the reader, it will be necessary to give the inaudible part of the conversation.

The two seated themselves in their basket-chairs, and Jim Armine lit a cigarette. There was a small lamp by him, the flame of which burned steadily in the still air. It cast a square of brilliant light into the courtyard beyond, across which, as across a magic-lantern sheet, white moths wandered from time to time, losing themselves again in the surrounding dark. There were several moments' silence, and then he looked at Eva, half of whose face was in brilliant illumination, and said,—

'You look tired to-night.'

'No, I am not tired,' she said, 'but I am feeling blank. Just now everything appears to me extremely uninteresting. I know from experience that things are not uninteresting really, and that is the worst of it. They are there, but I cannot touch them. I live in a grey fog; there is sunshine somewhere, quite close, but I cannot get to it. What else could I expect?'

Jim was attending eagerly.

'Of course I mayn't say how sorry I am for you,' he said in a low voice.

Eva did not turn her head, but the least sparkle returned to her eyes. Perhaps things were going to be amusing, after all, for a few minutes.

'I am grateful, of course,' she said. 'One is to be pitied when the fog is so palpably dense. Of course, it will lift again; fogs don't last for ever. I am glad you are with us, though I don't think you ought to be. After all, nothing matters much.'

Lord Hayes had by this time successfully focussed his ear to the indistinct sounds, and Eva's last remark was perfectly audible.

'Ah! but things *do* matter,' said the young man earnestly. 'And all men are not like some men.'

'By which I suppose you mean me to understand that you are not like some men. How can I know that? You have no halo round your head, no dawning of ineffable joy in your face. Why should I suppose you are more than others? You have spoken to me before now of your great aims, your enthusiasms for great causes, by which, as far as I know, you only mean Home Rule, or the Unionist policy—I forget what your politics are—and even that seems to have been in abeyance lately. You have been with us a week or more, and what have you done, what have you thought about? You seem to prefer, after all, talking to me—'

'You are very cruel, Eva,' said he.

Lord Hayes shut his window. Perhaps the night air was unwholesome after all. In any case, he had heard enough. Suspicion was running down the avenue, and growing clearer at every step. He hesitated a moment, and then left his room and walked downstairs. As he came out into the courtyard he heard the echo of Eva's light, cruel laughter.

Jim Armine was standing in front of her, with his arms hanging listlessly by his side. He did not look exactly happy, and the sight of Lord Hayes only added a very slightly deeper shade to his face.

Eva's husband never felt more methodically cool in his life. He had quite determined what to do. She had not seen him approach, and a smile still lingered on her lips. She was lying back in her chair, in indolent languor; only in her eyes was amusement and excitement.

'You looked very fine just then,' she was saying to Jim, and turning, she saw her husband.

The smile died off her lips, the amusement from her eyes. Only that air of utter languor was left. But she saw her vengeance coming near, as Lord Hayes had seen suspicion, and she met it joyfully.

Lord Hayes laid his hand on the young man's shoulder.

'The steamers only go twice a week to Marseilles,' he said, 'and there will be no steamer to-morrow. In the meantime, I am sure you will see the advisability of your spending the next two nights at the Hotel St George. They say it is a very good hotel. Of course we shall not receive callers.'

Eva shifted her position slightly, and looked at her husband.

'Kindly explain why he should go off so suddenly,' she said.

'I would not insult you by doing so.'

'The insult lies in your silence. I suppose you overheard something.'

'Yes,' said her husband. 'I was listening.'

'Ah! that is so like you. What were you listening for?'

'I was listening more or less for what I heard.'

'In fact, you suspected something of the sort?'

'Yes.'

'And yet you did not warn me. Go away, Mr Armine, and don't listen, please. Sit down, Hayes; I wish to talk to you. What a lovely night it is. Quite idyllic. By the way, I wish to know whether your suspicions are entirely confined to him.'

'Absolutely and entirely.'

'You are quite sure?'

'Quite.'

'That is good,' said Eva. 'But naturally I wanted to know. To return—why did you not warn me?'

Lord Hayes found that things were not going exactly as he had foreseen.

'I did not think it would be of any use to warn you,' he said at length.

'Then, as you have no suspicions whatever of me, what purpose is served by his going away?'

'His presence here, under this roof, is an insult to you and me.'

'Yet you did not warn me,' said Eva. 'It seems to me that you have cancelled the insult to yourself. Shall I tell you exactly what has happened, or do you know it all?'

'I know enough,' he said.

'Possibly, from your point of view. But I am afraid you must have left your box before the end. The end was important. How much did you hear exactly? However, it doesn't matter. He said something—well, extremely ill-judged, and I told him he had mistaken me altogether. I laughed as well. Did you hear me laugh? I said I had not the slightest doubt of his devotion, but that I did not feel the least inclined to accept it. I don't appreciate devotion, except my husband's, of course.'

Eva waited a moment. A refined cruelty waits

a little every now and then for the full effect of
the pain to be felt.

'It is impossible that he should remain here,'
he said.

'Please listen to me a moment. I have not
finished yet. You have insulted me grossly, twice ;
in the first place, by not warning me, in the second,
by listening. I do not like insults in the least,
and I have no intention of receiving them. Jim
committed an extreme indiscretion, for which you
are mainly responsible. If you had spoken to him
or me before, this would not have happened. Again,
if you had not listened, you would have known
nothing of it, and you will be good enough to take
my word for it, that no one would have been the
worse. He would have learnt a lesson, and I should
have had the pleasure of teaching it him. I did
not expect this in the least, for I did not think he
would have been so foolish as to speak of it.'

The degradation which her husband would have
imposed on her grew more and more bitter. She
stood up with intense anger intensely repressed.

'I choose that he should stop,' she said. 'I de-
spise you for listening. If you like, you may insist

on his going, and, if you do, I shall go too. I tell
you I am perfectly reckless, and perfectly determined. Your point is that I have been insulted.
It was you who insulted me by not giving me
warning, and if you play the spy on me in this
way, I owe you absolutely nothing. That is all.
You may choose ; and choose quickly.'

She waited a moment, giving him time to reply.

'Apparently you have nothing to say. In fact,
there is nothing for you to say. That is all, then.
If you are going to sit out here with us, you had
better tell them to bring you a chair. Understand
me quite clearly ; it is over. I shall never allude
to this again, and I must ask you not to, either.'

Lord Hayes walked away without saying a word.
Eva stood still one moment, steadying herself, and
then she called out to Jim, who was leaning against
a pillar at the opposite corner of the court.

'You can come back,' she said. 'We are not
going to send you away. Let us go on talking
from the last remark but two.'

She settled herself again in her chair and laughed.
The evening had been unexpectedly amusing.

'He will not listen again, and you will not talk

nonsense again, I hope. Really, this is an unique
position, and I am the only one of the three who
comes out of it with credit. *A* suspects that *B*, his
friend, is making love to his wife. Does not warn
her, but listens, and hears something that confirms
his suspicions. Tries to drive *B* out of the house.
They all meet amicably at breakfast next morning.'

Certainly, if Eva had felt she had any small score
to wipe off against her husband, she had wiped it
off very cleanly. He was, for those few moments
when she had stood up with her intense anger
thoroughly in hand, mortally afraid of her, and
she knew it. She had used her anger as a weapon
against him, and had not let it act wildly, or un-
premeditatedly. She well knew that, as a weapon,
anger is most useful when it is skilfully handled,
controlled, compressed. A horse without a rider,
lashed into the enemies' lines, may, it is true, do
some service by promiscuous kicking, but it is a
blind, ungoverned force ; a skilful rider, however, who
adapts its savage strength to his own intelligence,
can guide it and direct it, and its destructive
potentialities are increased tenfold.

It was as a serviceable though savage brute that

N

Eva employed her anger against her husband; she spurred it and lashed it into fury, but never gave it its head. That cruel, governed anger of women is a very terrible thing; the hot, blustering anger of a man is like a squib that bursts and jumps here and there, sometimes singeing its immediate surroundings and, perhaps, breaking something, but it wastes its force in childish, cracker-like explosions that hurt nothing but sensitive nerves, which regard such exhibitions as a lamentable want of taste. But Eva's anger could not have offended the most fastidious; it gave no annoying little bangs, no unexpected leaps, no fizzing, no unmomentous crackling; it was still, deep, intense, not pleasant to fight with.

Eva and Jim sat in the little courtyard for some half-hour more, which was rather a hard burden for the young man. To Eva it appeared to be no effort to talk as usual. She had required just one moment in which to steady herself, to dismount her quivering, indignant steed, and then for her, as she had told her husband, it was over. She had been angry, furious, insulted, and she had used the whip with a vengeance. The offence and the punishment were past, and she threw the whip into a corner.

But Jim was silent, which was not altogether un-
natural. He had no taste for scenes, and his great
coup, his ace of trumps, which, to his shame, had been
forced from him, seemed to have fallen very flat.
He had played it, and Eva had seen it, but that was
all—it had simply been wasted. Naturally enough
he felt he had spoiled his hand. Eva had laughed
at him, but she had not been offended. Surely such
an attitude was almost unprecedented.

When she went upstairs half an hour later, she
turned into her husband's room to get a book she
wanted, and found him sitting by the window, as
if expecting her. He rose as she entered, and stood
like a servant waiting for orders. But Eva gave
no orders, and, having found her book, only remarked that it was growing a little chilly. He did
not reply, and she turned to look at him. There
was something miserably shrunken about his appearance which was rather pitiful.

'You look tired,' she said. 'I should go to bed
if I were you.'

He did not meet her eyes, but continued to look
out of the window.

'It has been a terrible night,' he said.

Eva frowned.

'It has been nothing of the sort,' she said. 'Don't be absurd, Hayes. You made a very bad mistake; you did not treat me in the way I wish to be treated, and I was intensely angry with you. But I assure you I am angry no longer. It is quite over, as far as I am concerned. Don't let us quarrel more than is necessary. Just now, it is quite unnecessary to quarrel.'

Lord Hayes had a certain potentiality for being malignant.

'It is not the quarrelling,' he said; 'it is the mutual position that I find we occupy to each other.'

She grew a little impatient.

'Let that be enough,' she said. 'We only waste words.'

She came a step nearer to him, and laid her hand on his shoulder, as if he had been a woman, or she a man.

'Come,' she said, 'be sensible. There is nothing more to say about it. You had better go to bed. Good-night!'

END OF VOL. I.

A LIST OF NEW BOOKS
AND ANNOUNCEMENTS OF
METHUEN AND COMPANY
PUBLISHERS : LONDON
18 BURY STREET
W.C.

CONTENTS

OCTOBER 1893

MESSRS. METHUEN'S
ANNOUNCEMENTS

———◆———

Gladstone. THE SPEECHES AND PUBLIC ADDRESSES OF THE RT. HON. W. E. GLADSTONE, M.P. With Notes. Edited by A. W. HUTTON, M.A. (Librarian of the Gladstone Library), and H. J. COHEN, M.A. With Portraits. *8vo. Vol. IX.* 12s. 6d.

Messrs. METHUEN beg to announce that they are about to issue, in ten volumes 8vo, an authorised collection of Mr. Gladstone's Speeches, the work being undertaken with his sanction and under his superintendence. Notes and Introductions will be added.

In view of the interest in the Home Rule Question, it is proposed to issue Vols. IX. and X., which will include the speeches of the last seven or eight years, immediately, and then to proceed with the earlier volumes. Volume X. is already published.

Henley & Whibley. A BOOK OF ENGLISH PROSE. Collected by W. E. HENLEY and CHARLES WHIBLEY. *Crown 8vo.*

Also small limited editions on Dutch and Japanese paper. 21s. and 42s. *net.*

A companion book to Mr. Henley's well-known *Lyra Heroica.* It is believed that no such collection of splendid prose has ever been brought within the compass of one volume. Each piece, whether containing a character-sketch or incident, is complete in itself. The book will be finely printed and bound.

Henley. ENGLISH LYRICS. Selected and Edited by W. E. HENLEY. In Two Editions:

A limited issue on hand-made paper. *Large crown 8vo.*

A small issue on finest large Japanese paper. *Demy 8vo.*

The announcement of this important collection of English Lyrics will excite wide interest. It will be finely printed by Messrs. Constable & Co., and issued at first in limited editions.

Dixon. ENGLISH POETRY FROM BLAKE TO BROWNING. By W. M. DIXON, M.A. *Crown 8vo.* 5s.

A Popular Account of the Poetry of the Century.

Prior. CAMBRIDGE SERMONS. Edited by C. H. PRIOR, M.A., Fellow and Tutor of Pembroke College. *Crown 8vo.* 6s.

A volume of sermons preached before the University of Cambridge by various preachers, including the Archbishop of Canterbury and Bishop Westcott.

Oscar Browning. GUELPHS AND GHIBELLINES: A Short History of Mediæval Italy, A.D. 1250-1409. By OSCAR BROWNING, Fellow and Tutor of King's College, Cambridge. *Crown 8vo.* 5s.

O'Grady. THE STORY OF IRELAND. By STANDISH O'GRADY, Author of 'Finn and His Companions.' *Small crown 8vo.*

A short sketch of Irish History, simply and picturesquely told, for young people.

Scott. THE MAGIC HOUSE AND OTHER VERSES. By DUNCAN C. SCOTT. *Extra Post 8vo, bound in buckram.* 5s.

Lock. THE LIFE OF JOHN KEBLE. By WALTER LOCK, M.A. With Portrait from a painting by GEORGE RICHMOND, R.A. *Crown 8vo., buckram,* 5s. *Fifth Edition just ready.*

'A fine portrait ot one of the most saintly characters of our age, and a valuable contribution to the history of that Oxford Movement.'—*Times.*

Classical Translations

Irwin. LUCIAN—Six Dialogues (Nigrinus, Icaro-Menippus, Cock, Ship, Parasite, Law of Falsehood). Translated into English by S. T. IRWIN, M.A., Assistant Master at Clifton; late Scholar of Lincoln College, Oxford. *Crown 8vo.*

Morshead. SOPHOCLES—Electra and Ajax. Translated into English by E. D. A. MORSHEAD, M.A., late Scholar of New College, Oxford; Assistant Master at Winchester. *Crown 8vo.*

Two new volumes of the 'Classical Translations' series.

Fiction

Corelli. BARABBAS: A DREAM OF THE WORLD'S TRAGEDY. By MARIE CORELLI, Author of 'A Romance of Two Worlds,' 'Vendetta,' etc. 3 vols. *Crown 8vo.* 31s. 6d.

Baring Gould. CHEAP JACK ZITA. By S. BARING GOULD, Author of 'Mehalah,' 'In the Roar of the Sea,' etc. 3 vols., *Crown 8vo.* 31s. 6d.

A Romance of the Ely Fen District in 1815.

Fenn. THE STAR GAZERS. By G. MANVILLE FENN, Author of 'Eli's Children,' etc. 3 vols. *Crown 8vo.* 31s. 6d.

Esmé Stuart. A WOMAN OF FORTY. By ESMÉ STUART, Author of 'Muriel's Marriage,' 'Virginié's Husband,' etc. 2 vols. *Crown 8vo.* 21s.

Parker. THE TRANSLATION OF A SAVAGE. By
GILBERT PARKER, Author of 'Pierre and His People,' 'Mrs.
Falchion,' etc. *Crown 8vo.* 5*s.*
A picturesque story with a pathetic and original motive, by an author whose rise in
the estimation of the critics and the public has been rapid.

Gilchrist. THE STONE DRAGON. By MURRAY GILCHRIST.
Crown 8vo. Buckram, 6*s.*
A volume of stories of power so weird and original as to ensure them a ready welcome.

Benson. DODO: A DETAIL OF THE DAY. By E. F.
BENSON. *Crown 8vo. Seventh Edition.* 2 *vols.* 21*s.*
A story of society by a new writer, full of interest and power, which has already
passed through six editions, and has attracted by its brilliance universal attention. The best critics were cordial in their praise. The 'Guardian' spoke of
Dodo as *unusually clever and interesting*; the 'Spectator' called it *a delightfully witty sketch of society*; the 'Speaker' said the dialogue was *a perpetual
feast of epigram and paradox*; the 'Athenæum' spoke of the author as *a writer
of quite exceptional ability*; the 'Academy' praised his *amazing cleverness*; the
'World' said the book was *brilliantly written*; and half-a-dozen papers declared
there was *not a dull page in the two volumes.*

FOR BOYS AND GIRLS

Baring Gould. THE ICELANDER'S SWORD. By S.
BARING GOULD, Author of 'Mehalah,' etc. With twenty-nine
Illustrations by J. MOYR SMITH. *Crown 8vo.* 6*s.*
A stirring story of Iceland, written for boys by the author of ' In the Roar of the Sea.'

Cuthell. TWO LITTLE CHILDREN AND CHING. By
EDITH E. CUTHELL. Profusely Illustrated. *Crown 8vo. Cloth,
gilt edges,* 6*s.*
Another story, with a dog hero, by the author of the very popular 'Only a Guard-
Room Dog.'

Blake. TODDLEBEN'S HERO. By M. M. BLAKE, Author of
'The Siege of Norwich Castle.' With 36 Illustrations. *Crown
8vo.* 5*s.*
A story of military life for children.

NEW AND CHEAPER EDITIONS

Baring Gould. MRS. CURGENVEN OF CURGENVEN.
By S. BARING GOULD, Author of 'Mehalah,' 'Old Country Life,'
etc. *Crown 8vo. Third Edition.* 6*s.*
A powerful and characteristic story of Devon life by the author of 'Mehalah,' which
in its 3 vol. form passed through two editions. The 'Graphic' speaks of it as *a
novel of vigorous humour and sustained power*; the 'Sussex Daily News' says
that *the swing of the narrative is splendid*; and the 'Speaker' mentions its
bright imaginative power.

Parker. MRS. FALCHION. By GILBERT PARKER, Author of 'Pierre and His People.' *New Edition in one volume.* 6s.

Mr. Parker's second book has received a warm welcome. The 'Athenæum' called it *a splendid study of character*; the 'Pall Mall Gazette' spoke of the writing as *but little behind anything that has been done by any writer of our time*; the 'St. James'' called it *a very striking and admirable novel*; and the 'Westminster Gazette' applied to it the epithet of *distinguished.*

Norris. HIS GRACE. By W. E. NORRIS, Author of 'Mademoiselle de Mersac,' 'The Rogue,' etc. *Third and Cheaper Edition. Crown 8vo.* 6s.

An edition in one volume of a novel which in its two volume form quickly ran through two editions.

Pearce. JACO TRELOAR. By J. H. PEARCE, Author of 'Esther Pentreath.' *New Edition. Crown 8vo.* 3s. 6d.

A tragic story of Cornish life by a writer of remarkable power, whose first novel has been highly praised by Mr. Gladstone.

The 'Spectator' speaks of Mr. Pearce as *a writer of exceptional power*; the 'Daily Telegraph' calls it *powerful and picturesque*; the 'Birmingham Post' asserts that it is *a novel of high quality.*

Pryce. TIME AND THE WOMAN. By RICHARD PRYCE, Author of 'Miss Maxwell's Affections,' 'The Quiet Mrs. Fleming,' etc. *New and Cheaper Edition. Crown 8vo.* 6s.

'Mr. Pryce's work recalls the style of Octave Feuillet, by its clearness, conciseness, its literary reserve.'—*Athenæum.*

'It is impossible to read the book without interest and admiration.'—*Scotsman.*

'He has, in fact, written a book of some distinction, and the more his readers have thought and observed for themselves the more are they likely to appreciate it.'—*Pall Mall Gazette.*

'Quite peculiar fascination is exercised by this novel. The story is told with unusual cleverness. 'Time and the Woman' has genuine literary distinction, and the rarity of this quality in the ordinary novel needs no expression.'—*Vanity Fair.*

Dickenson. A VICAR'S WIFE. By EVELYN DICKENSON. *Cheap Edition. Crown 8vo.* 3s. 6d.

Prowse. THE POISON OF ASPS. By R. ORTON PROWSE. *Cheap Edition. Crown 8vo.* 3s. 6d.

UNIVERSITY EXTENSION SERIES
NEW VOLUMES. Crown 8vo.

A MANUAL OF ELECTRICAL SCIENCE. By GEORGE J. BURCH, M.A. With numerous Illustrations. 3s.

A practical, popular, and full handbook.

THE CHEMISTRY OF FIRE. By M. M. PATTISON MUIR,
M.A. Illustrated. 2s. 6d.
An exposition of the Elementary Principles of Chemistry.

A TEXT-BOOK OF AGRICULTURAL BOTANY. By M.C.
POTTER, M.A., F.L.S. Illustrated. 3s. 6d.

THE VAULT OF HEAVEN. A Popular Introduction to
Astronomy. By R. A. GREGORY. With numerous Illustrations.
Crown 8vo. 2s. 6d.

METEOROLOGY. The Elements of Weather and Climate.
By H. N. DICKSON, F.R.S.E., F.R. Met. Soc. Illustrated. 2s. 6d.

SOCIAL QUESTIONS OF TO-DAY

NEW VOLUMES.

Crown 8vo, 2s. 6d.

WOMEN'S WORK. By LADY DILKE, MISS BULLEY, and
MISS ABRAHAM.

TRUSTS, POOLS AND CORNERS. As affecting Commerce
and Industry. By J. STEPHEN JEANS, M.R.I., F.S.S.

𝕰𝖉𝖚𝖈𝖆𝖙𝖎𝖔𝖓𝖆𝖑 𝕭𝖔𝖔𝖐𝖘

Davis. TACITI GERMANIA. Edited with Notes and Introduction. By R. F. DAVIS, M.A., Editor of the 'Agricola.'
Small crown 8vo.

Stedman. GREEK TESTAMENT SELECTIONS. Edited by
A. M. M. STEDMAN, M.A. *Third and Revised Edition. Fcap. 8vo.*
2s. 6d.

Stedman. A SHORTER GREEK PRIMER OF ACCI-
DENCE AND SYNTAX. By A. M. M. STEDMAN, M.A.
Crown 8vo.

Stedman. STEPS TO FRENCH. By A. M. M. STEDMAN,
M.A. 18mo.
An attempt to supply a very easy and very short book of French Lessons.

Stedman. THE HELVETIAN WAR. Edited with Notes
and Vocabulary by A. M. M. STEDMAN, M.A. 18mo. 1s.

Methuen's Commercial Series

Crown 8vo.   Cloth.

Gibbins. BRITISH COMMERCE AND COLONIES FROM ELIZABETH TO VICTORIA. By H. DE B. GIBBINS, M.A., Author of 'The Industrial History of England,' etc., etc.   2*s*.

Bally. A MANUAL OF FRENCH COMMERCIAL CORRESPONDENCE. By S. E. BALLY, Modern Language Master at the Manchester Grammar School.

Lyde. COMMERCIAL GEOGRAPHY, with special reference to Trade Routes, New Markets, and Manufacturing Districts. By L. D. LYDE, M.A., of The Academy, Glasgow.   2*s*.

Simplified Classics

A series of Classical Readers, Edited for Lower Forms with Introductions, Notes, Maps, and Illustrations.

Herodotus. THE PERSIAN WARS. Edited by A. G. LIDDELL, M.A., Assistant Master at Nottingham High School.

Plautus. THE CAPTIVI. Edited by J. H. FREESE, M.A., late Fellow of St. John's College, Cambridge.

Livy. THE KINGS OF ROME. Edited by A. M. M. STEDMAN, M.A.

Methuen's Novel Series

A Series of copyright Novels, by well-known Authors, bound in red buckram, at the price of three shillings and sixpence. The first volumes will be :— **3/6**

1. JACQUETTA. By S. BARING GOULD, Author of ' Mehalah', etc.

2. ARMINELL: A Social Romance. By S. BARING GOULD, Author of ' Mehalah,' etc.

3. MARGERY OF QUETHER. By S. BARING GOULD.

4. URITH. By S. BARING GOULD.

5. IN THE ROAR OF THE SEA. By S. BARING GOULD.

6. DERRICK VAUGHAN, NOVELIST. With Portrait of Author. By EDNA LYALL, Author of 'Donovan,' etc.

7. JACK'S FATHER. By W. E. NORRIS.

8. MY DANISH SWEETHEART. By W. CLARK RUSSELL.

HALF-CROWN NOVELS.

A Series of Novels by popular Authors, tastefully bound in cloth.   **2/6**

1. THE PLAN OF CAMPAIGN. By F. MABEL ROBINSON.

2. DISENCHANTMENT. By F. MABEL ROBINSON.

3. MR. BUTLER'S WARD. By MABEL ROBINSON.

4. HOVENDEN, V.C. By F. MABEL ROBINSON.

5. ELI'S CHILDREN. By G. MANVILLE FENN.

6. A DOUBLE KNOT. By G. MANVILLE FENN.

7. DISARMED. By M. BETHAM EDWARDS.

8. A LOST ILLUSION. By LESLIE KEITH.

9. A MARRIAGE AT SEA. By W. CLARK RUSSELL.

10. IN TENT AND BUNGALOW. By the Author of 'Indian Idylls.'

11. MY STEWARDSHIP. By E. M'QUEEN GRAY.

12. A REVEREND GENTLEMAN. By J. M. COBBAN.

13. THE STORY OF CHRIS. By ROWLAND GREY.

Other Volumes will be announced in due course.

Books for Girls

A Series of Books by well-known Authors, bound uniformly.

Walford. A PINCH OF EXPERIENCE. By L. B. WAL-FORD, Author of 'Mr. Smith.' With Illustrations by GORDON BROWNE. *Crown 8vo.* 3*s.* 6*d.*

'The clever authoress steers clear of namby-pamby, and invests her moral with a fresh and striking dress. There is terseness and vivacity of style, and the illustrations are admirable.'—*Anti-Jacobin.*

Molesworth. THE RED GRANGE. By Mrs. MOLESWORTH, Author of 'Carrots.' With Illustrations by GORDON BROWNE. *Crown 8vo.* 3s. 6d.

'A volume in which girls will delight, and beautifully illustrated.'—*Pall Mall Gazette.*

Author of 'Mdle. Mori.' THE SECRET OF MADAME DE Monluc. By the Author of 'The Atelier du Lys,' 'Mdle. Mori.' *Crown 8vo.* 3s. 6d.

'An exquisite literary cameo.'—*World.*

Parr. DUMPS. By Mrs. PARR, Author of 'Adam and Eve,' 'Dorothy Fox,' etc. Illustrated by W. PARKINSON. *Crown 8vo.* 3s. 6d.

'One of the prettiest stories which even this clever writer has given the world for a long time.'—*World.*

Meade. OUT OF THE FASHION. By L. T. MEADE, Author of 'A Girl of the People,' etc. With 6 Illustrations by W. PAGET. *Crown 8vo.* 3s. 6d.   .

'One of those charmingly-written social tales, which this writer knows so well how to write. It is delightful reading, and is well illustrated by W. Paget.'—*Glasgow Herald.*

Meade. A GIRL OF THE PEOPLE. By L. T. MEADE, Author of 'Scamp and I,' etc. Illustrated by R. BARNES. *Crown 8vo.* 3s. 6d.

'An excellent story. Vivid portraiture of character, and broad and wholesome lessons about life.'—*Spectator.*

'One of Mrs. Meade's most fascinating books.'—*Daily News.*

Meade. HEPSY GIPSY. By L. T. MEADE. Illustrated by EVERARD HOPKINS. *Crown 8vo.* 2s. 6d.

'Mrs. Meade has not often done better work than this.'—*Spectator.*

Meade. THE HONOURABLE MISS: A Tale of a Country Town. By L. T. MEADE, Author of 'Scamp and I,' 'A Girl of the People,' etc. With Illustrations by EVERARD HOPKINS. *Crown 8vo.* 3s. 6d.

Adams. MY LAND OF BEULAH. By MRS. LEITH ADAMS. With a Frontispiece by GORDON BROWNE. *Crown 8vo.* 3s. 6d.

A 2

𝔑ew and 𝔑ecent 𝔅ooks

Poetry

Rudyard Kipling. BARRACK-ROOM BALLADS; And Other Verses. By RUDYARD KIPLING. *Sixth Edition. Crown 8vo. 6s.*

A Special Presentation Edition, bound in white buckram, with extra gilt ornament. *7s. 6d.*

'Mr. Kipling's verse is strong, vivid, full of character. . . . Unmistakable genius rings in every line.'—*Times.*

'The disreputable lingo of Cockayne is henceforth justified before the world; for a man of genius has taken it in hand, and has shown, beyond all cavilling, that in its way it also is a medium for literature. You are grateful, and you say to yourself, half in envy and half in admiration: '' Here is a *book*; here, or one is a Dutchman, is one of the books of the year.'' '—*National Observer.*

' '' Barrack-Room Ballads ' contains some of the best work that Mr. Kipling has ever done, which is saying a good deal. '' Fuzzy-Wuzzy,'' ''Gunga Din,'' and '' Tommy,'' are, in our opinion. altogether superior to anything of the kind that English literature has hitherto produced.'—*Athenæum*

'These ballads are as wonderful in their descriptive power as they are vigorous in their dramatic force. There are few ballads in the English language more stirring than ''The Ballad of East and West,'' worthy to stand by the Border ballads of Scott.'—*Spectator.*

'The ballads teem with imagination, they palpitate with emotion. We read them with laughter and tears; the metres throb in our pulses, the cunningly ordered words tingle with life; and if this be not poetry, what is?'—*Pall Mall Gazette.*

Henley. LYRA HEROICA: An Anthology selected from the best English Verse of the 16th, 17th, 18th, and 19th Centuries. By WILLIAM ERNEST HENLEY, Author of ' A Book of Verse,' ' Views and Reviews,' etc. *Crown 8vo. Stamped gilt buckram, gilt top, edges uncut. 6s.*

Mr. Henley has brought to the task of selection an instinct alike for poetry and for chivalry which seems to us quite wonderfully, and even unerringly, right.'—*Guardian.*

Tomson. A SUMMER NIGHT, AND OTHER POEMS. By GRAHAM R. TOMSON. With Frontispiece by A. TOMSON. *Fcap. 8vo. 3s. 6d.*

Also an edition on hand-made paper, limited to 50 copies. *Large crown 8vo. 10s. 6d. net.*

' Mrs. Tomson holds perhaps the very highest rank among poetesses of English birth. This selection will help her reputation.'—*Black and White.*

Ibsen. BRAND. A Drama by HENRIK IBSEN. Translated by
WILLIAM WILSON. *Crown 8vo.* 5*s.*
'The greatest world-poem of the nineteenth century next to "Faust." "Brand"
will have an astonishing interest for Englishmen. It is in the same set with
"Agamemnon," with "Lear," with the literature that we now instinctively regard
as high and holy.'—*Daily Chronicle.*

'Q.'' GREEN BAYS : Verses and Parodies. By " Q.," Author
of 'Dead Man's Rock ' etc. *Second Edition. Fcap. 8vo.* 3*s.* 6*d.*
'The verses display a rare and versatile gift of parody, great command of metre, and
a very pretty turn of humour.'—*Times.*

"A. G." VERSES TO ORDER. By "A. G." *Crown 8vo,*
cloth extra, gilt top. 2*s.* 6*d. net.*
A small volume of verse by a writer whose initials are well known to Oxford men.
'A capital specimen of light academic poetry. These verses are very bright and
engaging, easy and sufficiently witty.'—*St. James's Gazette.*

Hosken. VERSES BY THE WAY. By J. D. HOSKEN.
Printed on laid paper, and bound in buckram, gilt top. 5*s.*
Also a small edition on large Dutch hand-made paper. *Price*
12*s.* 6*d. net.*
A Volume of Lyrics and Sonnets by J. D. Hosken, the Postman Poet, of Helston,
Cornwall, whose interesting career is now more or less well known to the literary
public. Q, the Author of 'The Splendid Spur,' etc., writes a critical and
biographical introduction.

Langbridge. A CRACKED FIDDLE. Being Selections from
the Poems of FREDERIC LANGBRIDGE. With Portrait. *Crown 8vo.* 5*s.*

Langbridge. BALLADS OF THE BRAVE : Poems of Chivalry
Enterprise, Courage, and Constancy, from the Earliest Times to the
Present Day. Edited, with Notes, by Rev. F. LANGBRIDGE.
Crown 8vo. Buckram 3*s.* 6*d.* School Edition, 2*s.* 6*d.*
'A very happy conception happily carried out. These "Ballads of the Brave" are
intended to suit the real tastes of boys, and will suit the taste of the great majority.'
—*Spectator.*   ' The book is full of splendid things.'—*World.*

History and Biography

Collingwood. JOHN RUSKIN: His Life and Work. By
W. G. COLLINGWOOD, M.A., late Scholar of University College,
Oxford, Author of the 'Art Teaching of John Ruskin,' Editor of
Mr. Ruskin's Poems. 2 *vols.* 8*vo.* 32*s. Second Edition.*
This important work is written by Mr. Collingwood, who has been for some years
Mr. Ruskin's private secretary, and who has had unique advantages in obtaining

materials for this book from Mr. Ruskin himself and from his friends. It contains a large amount of new matter, and of letters which have never been published, and is, in fact, a full and authoritative biography of Mr. Ruskin. The book contains numerous portraits of Mr. Ruskin, including a coloured one from a water-colour portrait by himself, and also 13 sketches, never before published, by Mr. Ruskin and Mr. Arthur Severn. A bibliography is added.

'No more magnificent volumes have been published for a long time than "The Life and Work of John Ruskin." . . .'—*Times.*

'This most lovingly written and most profoundly interesting book.'—*Daily News.*

'It is long since we have had a biography with such varied delights of substance and of form. Such a book is a pleasure for the day, and a joy for ever.'—*Daily Chronicle.*

'Mr. Ruskin could not well have been more fortunate in his biographer.'—*Globe.*

'A noble monument of a noble subject. One of the most beautiful books about one of the noblest lives of our century.'—*Glasgow Herald.*

Gladstone. THE SPEECHES AND PUBLIC ADDRESSES OF THE RT. HON. W. E. GLADSTONE, M.P. With Notes and Introductions. Edited by A. W. HUTTON, M.A. (Librarian of the Gladstone Library), and H. J. COHEN, M.A. With Portraits. *8vo. Vol. X. 12s. 6d.*

Russell. THE LIFE OF ADMIRAL LORD COLLING-WOOD. By W. CLARK RUSSELL, Author of 'The Wreck of the Grosvenor.' With Illustrations by F. BRANGWYN. *8vo. 15s.*

'A really good book.'—*Saturday Review.*

'A most excellent and wholesome book, which we should like to see in the hands of every boy in the country.'—*St. James's Gazette.*

Clark. THE COLLEGES OF OXFORD: Their History and their Traditions. By Members of the University. Edited by A. CLARK, M.A., Fellow and Tutor of Lincoln College. *8vo. 12s. 6d.*

'Whether the reader approaches the book as a patriotic member of a college, as an antiquary, or as a student of the organic growth of college foundation, it will amply reward his attention.'—*Times.*

'A delightful book, learned and lively. —*Academy.*

'A work which will certainly be appealed to for many years as the standard book on the Colleges of Oxford.'—*Athenæum.*

Hulton. RIXAE OXONIENSES: An Account of the Battles of the Nations, The Struggle between Town and Gown, etc. By S. F. HULTON, M.A. *Crown 8vo. 5s.*

James. CURIOSITIES OF CHRISTIAN HISTORY PRIOR TO THE REFORMATION. By CROAKE JAMES, Author of 'Curiosities of Law and Lawyers.' *Crown 8vo. 7s. 6d.*

Perrens. THE HISTORY OF FLORENCE FROM THE TIME OF THE MEDICIS TO THE FALL OF THE REPUBLIC. By F. T. PERRENS. Translated by HANNAH LYNCH. In three volumes. *Vol. I. 8vo.* 12s. 6d.

This is a translation from the French of the best history of Florence in existence. This volume covers a period of profound interest—political and literary—and is written with great vivacity.

'This is a standard book by an honest and intelligent historian, who has deserved well of his countrymen, and of all who are interested in Italian history.'—*Manchester Guardian.*

Kaufmann. CHARLES KINGSLEY. By M. KAUFMANN, M.A. *Crown 8vo.* 5s.

A biography of Kingsley, especially dealing with his achievements in social reform.

'The author has certainly gone about his work with conscientiousness and industry.'—*Sheffield Daily Telegraph.*

Oliphant. THOMAS CHALMERS: A Biography. By Mrs. OLIPHANT. With Portrait. *Crown 8vo. Buckram,* 5s.

'A well-executed biography, worthy of its author and of the remarkable man who is its subject. Mrs. Oliphant relates lucidly and dramatically the important part which Chalmers played in the memorable secession.'—*Times.*

'Written with all the facile literary grace that marks this indefatigable authoress' work, it presents a very complete picture of Chalmers as he lived and worked. . . . The salient points in his many-sided life are seized with unerring judgment.'— *North British Daily Mail.*

Wells. THE TEACHING OF HISTORY IN SCHOOLS. A Lecture delivered at the University Extension Meeting in Oxford, Aug. 6th, 1892. By J. WELLS, M.A., Fellow and Tutor of Wadham College, and Editor of 'Oxford and Oxford Life.' *Crown 8vo.* 6d.

Pollard. THE JESUITS IN POLAND. By A. F. POLLARD, B.A. Oxford Prize Essays—The Lothian Prize Essay 1892. *Crown 8vo.* 2s. 6d. *net.*

Clifford. THE DESCENT OF CHARLOTTE COMPTON (BARONESS FERRERS DE CHARTLEY). By her Great-Granddaughter, ISABELLA G. C. CLIFFORD. *Small 4to.* 10s. 6d. *net.*

General Literature

Bowden. THE IMITATION OF BUDDHA: Being Quotations from Buddhist Literature for each Day in the Year. Compiled by E. M. BOWDEN. With Preface by Sir EDWIN ARNOLD. *Third Edition.* 16mo. 2s. 6d.

Ditchfield. OUR ENGLISH VILLAGES : Their Story and their Antiquities. By P. H. DITCHFIELD, M.A., F.R.H.S., Rector of Barkham, Berks. *Post 8vo.* 2s. 6d. Illustrated.

'An extremely amusing and interesting little book, which should find a place in every parochial library.'—*Guardian.*

Ditchfield. OLD ENGLISH SPORTS. By P. H. DITCH-FIELD, M.A. *Crown 8vo.* 2s. 6d. Illustrated.

'A charming account of old English Sports.'—*Morning Post.*

Burne. PARSON AND PEASANT : Chapters of their Natural History. By J. B. BURNE, M.A., Rector of Wasing. *Crown 8vo.* 5s.

'"Parson and Peasant" is a book not only to be interested in, but to learn something from—a book which may prove a help to many a clergyman, and broaden the hearts and ripen the charity of laymen.'—*Derby Mercury.*

Massee. A MONOGRAPH OF THE MYXOGASTRES. By GEORGE MASSEE. With 12 Coloured Plates. *Royal 8vo.* 18s. *net.*

This is the only work in English on this important group. It contains 12 Coloured Plates, produced in the finest style of chromo-lithography.

'Supplies a want acutely felt. Its merits are of a high order, and it is one of the most important contributions to systematic natural science which have lately appeared.'—*Westminster Review.*

'A work much in advance of any book in the language treating of this group or organisms. It is indispensable to every student of the Mxyogastres. The coloured plates deserve high praise for their accuracy and execution.'—*Nature.*

Cunningham. THE PATH TOWARDS KNOWLEDGE: Essays on Questions of the Day. By W. CUNNINGHAM, D.D., Fellow of Trinity College, Cambridge, Professor of Economics at King's College, London. *Crown 8vo.* 4s. 6d.

Essays on Marriage and Population, Socialism, Money, Education, Positivism, etc.

Bushill. PROFIT SHARING AND THE LABOUR QUES-TION. By T. W. BUSHILL, a Profit Sharing Employer. With an Introduction by SEDLEY TAYLOR, Author of ' Profit Sharing between Capital and Labour.' *Crown 8vo.* 2s. 6d.

John Beever. PRACTICAL FLY FISHING, Founded on Nature, by JOHN BEEVER, late of the Thwaite House, Coniston. A New Edition, with a Memoir of the Author by W. G. COLLINGWOOD, M.A., Author of 'The Life and Work of John Ruskin,' etc. Also additional Notes and a chapter on Char-Fishing, by A. and A. R. SEVERN. With a specially designed title-page. *Crown 8vo.* 3s. 6d.

A little book on Fly-Fishing by an old friend of Mr. Ruskin. It has been out of print for some time, and being still much in request, is now issued with a Memoir of the Author by W. G. Collingwood.

Anderson Graham. NATURE IN BOOKS : Studies in Literary Biography. By P. ANDERSON GRAHAM. *Crown 8vo.* 6s.

The chapters are entitled : I. ' The Magic of the Fields ' (Jefferies). II. 'Art and Nature ' (Tennyson). III. ' The Doctrine of Idleness ' (Thoreau). IV. 'The Romance of Life ' (Scott). V. ' The Poetry of Toil ' (Burns). VI. ' The Divinity of Nature ' (Wordsworth).

Wells. OXFORD AND OXFORD LIFE. By Members of the University. Edited by J. WELLS, M.A., Fellow and Tutor of Wadham College. *Crown 8vo.* 3s. 6d.

This work contains an account of life at Oxford—intellectual, social, and religious—a careful estimate of necessary expenses, a review of recent changes, a statement of the present position of the University, and chapters on Women's Education, aids to study, and University Extension.

'We congratulate Mr. Wells on the production of a readable and intelligent account of Oxford as it is at the present time, written by persons who are, with hardly an exception, possessed of a close acquaintance with the system and life of the University.'—*Athenæum.*

Driver. SERMONS ON SUBJECTS CONNECTED WITH THE OLD TESTAMENT. By S. R. DRIVER, D.D., Canon of Christ Church, Regius Professor of Hebrew in the University of Oxford. *Crown 8vo.* 6s.

A welcome volume to the author's famous ' Introduction.' No man can read these discourses without feeling that Dr. Driver is fully alive to the deeper teaching of the Old Testament.'—*Guardian.*

Cheyne. FOUNDERS OF OLD TESTAMENT CRITICISM: Biographical, Descriptive, and Critical Studies. By T. K. CHEYNE, D.D., Oriel Professor of the Interpretation of Holy Scripture at Oxford. *Large crown 8vo.* 7s. 6d. [*Ready.*

This important book is a historical sketch of O.T. Criticism in the form of biographical studies from the days of Eichhorn to those of Driver and Robertson Smith. It is the only book of its kind in English.

'The volume is one of great interest and value. It displays all the author's well-known ability and learning, and its opportune publication has laid all students of theology, and specially of Bible criticism, under weighty obligation.'—*Scotsman.*

' A very learned and instructive work.'—*Times.*

WORKS BY

S. Baring Gould, Author of 'Mehalah,' etc.

OLD COUNTRY LIFE. With Sixty-seven Illustrations by W. PARKINSON, F. D. BEDFORD, and F. MASEY. *Large Crown 8vo, cloth super extra, top edge gilt,* 10s. 6d. *Fourth and Cheaper Edition.* 6s.

'"Old Country Life," as healthy wholesome reading, full of breezy life and movement, full of quaint stories vigorously told, will not be excelled by any book to be published throughout the year. Sound, hearty, and English to the core.'—*World.*

HISTORIC ODDITIES AND STRANGE EVENTS. *Third Edition, Crown 8vo. 6s.*

'A collection of exciting and entertaining chapters. The whole volume is delightful reading.'—*Times.*

FREAKS OF FANATICISM. *Third Edition. Crown 8vo. 6s.*

'Mr. Baring Gould has a keen eye for colour and effect, and the subjects he has chosen give ample scope to his descriptive and analytic faculties. A perfectly fascinating book.'—*Scottish Leader.*

SONGS OF THE WEST: Traditional Ballads and Songs of the West of England, with their Traditional Melodies. Collected by S. BARING GOULD, M.A., and H. FLEETWOOD SHEPPARD, M.A. Arranged for Voice and Piano. In 4 Parts (containing 25 Songs each), *Parts I., II., III., 3s. each. Part IV., 5s. In one Vol., roan, 15s.*

'A rich and varied collection of humour, pathos, grace, and poetic fancy.'—*Saturday Review.*

YORKSHIRE ODDITIES AND STRANGE EVENTS. *Fourth Edition. Crown 8vo. 6s.*

STRANGE SURVIVALS AND SUPERSTITIONS. With Illustrations. By S. BARING GOULD. *Crown 8vo. 7s. 6d.*

A book on such subjects as Foundations, Gables, Holes, Gallows, Raising the Hat, Old Ballads, etc. etc. It traces in a most interesting manner their origin and history.
'We have read Mr. Baring Gould's book from beginning to end. It is full of quaint and various information, and there is not a dull page in it.'—*Notes and Queries.*

THE TRAGEDY OF THE CAESARS: The Emperors of the Julian and Claudian Lines. With numerous Illustrations from Busts, Gems, Cameos, etc. By S. BARING GOULD, Author of 'Mehalah,' etc. *Second Edition. 2 vols. Royal 8vo. 30s.*

This book is the only one in English which deals with the personal history of the Caesars, and Mr. Baring Gould has found a subject which, for picturesque detail and sombre interest, is not rivalled by any work of fiction. The volumes are copiously illustrated.
'A most splendid and fascinating book on a subject of undying interest. The great feature of the book is the use the author has made of the existing portraits of the Caesars, and the admirable critical subtlety he has exhibited in dealing with this line of research. It is brilliantly written, and the illustrations are supplied on a scale of profuse magnificence.'—*Daily Chronicle.*
'The volumes will in no sense disappoint the general reader. Indeed, in their way, there is nothing in any sense so good in English. . . . Mr. Baring Gould has presented his narrative in such a way as not to make one dull page.'—*Athenæum.*

JACQUETTA, and other Stories. *Crown 8vo. 3s. 6d.*

ARMINELL : A Social Romance. *New Edition. Crown 8vo.* 3*s*. 6*d*.
'To say that a book is by the author of "Mehalah" is to imply that it contains a story cast on strong lines, containing dramatic possibilities, vivid and sympathetic descriptions of Nature, and a wealth of ingenious imagery. All these expectations are justified by "Arminell."'—*Speaker.*

URITH : A Story of Dartmoor. *Third Edition. Crown 8vo.* 3*s*.6*d*.
'The author is at his best.'—*Times.*
'He has nearly reached the high water-mark of "Mehalah."'—*National Observer.*

MARGERY OF QUETHER, and other Stories. *Crown 8vo.* 3*s*. 6*d*.

IN THE ROAR OF THE SEA : A Tale of the Cornish Coast. *New Edition.* 3*s*. 6*d*.

MRS. CURGENVEN OF CURGENVEN. *Third Edition.* 6*s*.

Fiction

Pryce. TIME AND THE WOMAN. By RICHARD PRYCE, Author of 'Miss Maxwell's Affections,' 'The Quiet Mrs. Fleming,' etc. New and Cheaper Edition. *Crown 8vo.* 6*s*.
' Mr. Pryce's work recalls the style of Octave Feuillet, by its clearness, conciseness, its literary reserve.'—*Athenæum.*

Gray. ELSA. A Novel. By E. M'QUEEN GRAY. *Crown 8vo.* 6*s*.
'A charming novel. The characters are not only powerful sketches, but minutely and carefully finished portraits.'—*Guardian.*

Anthony Hope. A CHANGE OF AIR : A Novel. By ANTHONY HOPE, Author of ' Mr. Witt's Widow,' etc. 1 *vol. Crown 8vo.* 6*s*.
A bright story by Mr. Hope, who has, the *Athenæum* says, 'a decided outlook and individuality of his own.'
' A graceful, vivacious comedy, true to human nature. The characters are traced with a masterly hand.'—*Times.*

Edna Lyall. DERRICK VAUGHAN, NOVELIST. By EDNA LYALL, Author of ' Donovan.' *Crown 8vo.* 31*st Thousand.* 3*s*. 6*d*. ; *paper,* 1*s*.

Lynn Linton. THE TRUE HISTORY OF JOSHUA DAVIDSON, Christian and Communist. By E. LYNN LINTON. Eleventh Edition. *Post 8vo.* 1*s*.

Dicker. A CAVALIER'S LADYE. By CONSTANCE DICKER. With Illustrations. *Crown 8vo.* 3*s*. 6*d*.

Author of 'Vera.' THE DANCE OF THE HOURS. By the Author of ' Vera,' ' Blue Roses,' etc. *Crown 8vo.* 6s.

'A musician's dream, pathetically broken off at the hour of its realisation, is vividly represented in this book. . . . Well written and possessing many elements of interest. The success of "The Dance of the Hours" may be safely predicted.'— *Morning Post.*

Norris. A Deplorable Affair. By W. E. NORRIS, Author of 'His Grace.' *Crown 8vo.* 3s. 6d.

'What with its interesting story, its graceful manner, and its perpetual good humour, the book is as enjoyable as any that has come from its author's pen.'— *Scotsman.*

Dickinson. A VICAR'S WIFE. By EVELYN DICKINSON. *Crown 8vo.* 3s. 6d.

Prowse. THE POISON OF ASPS. By R. ORTON PROWSE. *Crown 8vo.* 3s. 6d.

Parker. PIERRE AND HIS PEOPLE. By GILBERT PARKER. *Crown 8vo.* *Buckram.* 6s.

'Stories happily conceived and finely executed. There is strength and genius in Mr. Parker's style.'—*Daily Telegraph.*

Marriott Watson. DIOGENES OF LONDON and other Sketches. By H. B. MARRIOTT WATSON, Author of ' The Web of the Spider.' *Crown 8vo.* *Buckram.* 6s.

' By all those who delight in the uses of words, who rate the exercise of prose above the exercise of verse, who rejoice in all proofs of its delicacy and its strength, who believe that English prose is chief among the moulds of thought, by these Mr. Marriott Watson's book will be welcomed.'—*National Observer.*

Methuen's Novel Series

A series of copyright Novels, by well-known Authors, bound in red buckram, at the price of three shillings and sixpence. The first volumes (ready) are :— 3/6

1. JACQUETTA. By S. BARING GOULD, Author of ' Mehalah,' etc.

2. ARMINELL : A Social Romance. By S. BARING GOULD, Author of ' Mehalah,' etc.

3. MARGERY OF QUETHER. By S. BARING GOULD.

4. URITH. By S. BARING GOULD.

5. IN THE ROAR OF THE SEA. By S. BARING GOULD.
6. DERRICK VAUGHAN, NOVELIST. With Portrait of Author. By EDNA LYALL, Author of 'Donovan,' etc. Also paper, 1s.
7. JACK'S FATHER. By W. E. NORRIS.
8. MY DANISH SWEETHEART. By W. CLARK RUSSELL.

Other Volumes will be announced in due course.

HALF-CROWN NOVELS

A Series of Novels by popular Authors, tastefully bound in cloth.   2/6

1. THE PLAN OF CAMPAIGN. By F. MABEL ROBINSON.
2. DISENCHANTMENT. By F. MABEL ROBINSON.
3. MR. BUTLER'S WARD. By MABEL ROBINSON.
4. HOVENDEN, V.C. By F. MABEL ROBINSON.
5. ELI'S CHILDREN. By G. MANVILLE FENN.
6. A DOUBLE KNOT. By G. MANVILLE FENN.
7. DISARMED. By M. BETHAM EDWARDS.
8. A LOST ILLUSION. By LESLIE KEITH.
9. A MARRIAGE AT SEA. By W. CLARK RUSSELL.
10. IN TENT AND BUNGALOW. By the Author of 'Indian Idylls.'
11. MY STEWARDSHIP. By E. M'QUEEN GRAY.
12. A REVEREND GENTLEMAN. By J. M. COBBAN.
13. THE STORY OF CHRIS. By ROLAND GREY.

Other volumes will be announced in due course.

NEW TWO-SHILLING EDITIONS

Crown 8vo, Ornamental Boards.   2/-

ELI'S CHILDREN. By G. MANVILLE FENN.
DISENCHANTMENT. By F. MABEL ROBINSON.
THE PLAN OF CAMPAIGN. By F. MABEL ROBINSON.

Crown 8vo.   Picture Boards.

A REVEREND GENTLEMAN.· By J. MacLaren Cobban.

MR. BUTLER'S WARD. By Mabel Robinson.

JACK'S FATHER. By W. E. Norris.

THE QUIET MRS. FLEMING. By Richard Pryce.

Books for Boys and Girls

Cuthell. ONLY A GUARD-ROOM DOG. By Mrs. Cuthell. With 16 Illustrations by W. Parkinson. *Square Crown 8vo.   6s.*

'This is a charming story. Tangle was but a little mongrel Skye terrier, but he had a big heart in his little body, and played a hero's part more than once. The book can be warmly recommended.'—*Standard.*

Collingwood. THE DOCTOR OF THE JULIET. By Harry Collingwood, Author of 'The Pirate Island,' etc. Illustrated by Gordon Browne. *Crown 8vo.   6s.*

'"The Doctor of the Juliet," well illustrated by Gordon Browne, is one of Harry Collingwood's best efforts.'—*Morning Post.*

Clark Russell. MASTER ROCKAFELLAR'S VOYAGE. By W. Clark Russell, Author of 'The Wreck of the Grosvenor,' etc. Illustrated by Gordon Browne. *Crown 8vo.   3s. 6d.*

'Mr. Clark Russell's story of "Master Rockafellar's Voyage" will be among the favourites of the Christmas books. There is a rattle and "go" all through it, and its illustrations are charming in themselves, and very much above the average in the way in which they are produced.'—*Guardian.*

Manville Fenn. SYD BELTON : Or, The Boy who would not go to Sea. By G. Manville Fenn, Author of 'In the King's Name,' etc. Illustrated by Gordon Browne. *Crown 8vo.   3s. 6d.*

'Who among the young story-reading public will not rejoice at the sight of the old combination, so often proved admirable—a story by Manville Fenn, Illustrated by Gordon Browne? The story, too, is one of the good old sort, full of life and vigour, breeziness and fun.'—*Journal of Education.*

Walford. A PINCH OF EXPERIENCE. By. L. B. Walford, Author of 'Mr. Smith.' With Illustrations by Gordon Browne. *Crown 8vo.   3s. 6d.*

'The clever authoress steers clear of namby-pamby, and invests her moral with a fresh and striking dress. There is terseness and vivacity of style and the illustrations are admirable.'—*Anti-Jacobin.*

Molesworth. THE RED GRANGE. By Mrs. MOLESWORTH, Author of 'Carrots.' With Illustrations by GORDON BROWNE. *Crown 8vo.* 3*s.* 6*d.*

'A volume in which girls will delight, and beautifully illustrated.'—*Pall Mall Gazette.*

Author of 'Mdle. Mori.' THE SECRET OF MADAME DE Monluc. By the Author of 'The Atelier du Lys,' 'Mdle. Mori.' *Crown 8vo.* 3*s.* 6*d.*

'An exquisite literary cameo.'—*World.*

Parr. DUMPS. By Mrs. PARR, Author of 'Adam and Eve,' 'Dorothy Fox,' etc. Illustrated by W. PARKINSON. *Crown 8vo.* 3*s.* 6*d.*

'One of the prettiest stories which even this clever writer has given the world for a long time.'—*World.*

Meade. OUT OF THE FASHION. By L. T. MEADE, Author of 'A Girl of the People,' etc. With 6 illustrations by W. PAGET. *Crown 8vo,* 3*s.* 6*d.*

'One of those charmingly-written social tales, which this writer knows so well how to write. It is delightful reading, and is well illustrated by W. Paget.'—*Glasgow Herald.*

Meade. A GIRL OF THE PEOPLE. By L. T. MEADE, Author of 'Scamp and I,' etc. Illustrated by R. BARNES. *Crown 8vo.* 3*s.* 6*d.*

'An excellent story. Vivid portraiture of character, and broad and wholesome lessons about life.'—*Spectator.*
'One of Mrs. Meade's most fascinating books.'—*Daily News.*

Meade. HEPSY GIPSY. By L. T. MEADE. Illustrated by EVERARD HOPKINS. *Crown 8vo.* 2*s.* 6*d.*

'Mrs. Meade has not often done better work than this.'—*Spectator.*

Meade. THE HONOURABLE MISS: A Tale of a Country Town. By L. T. MEADE, Author of 'Scamp and I,' 'A Girl of the People,' etc. With Illustrations by EVERARD HOPKINS. *Crown 8vo.* 3*s.* 6*d.*

Adams. MY LAND OF BEULAH. By Mrs. LEITH ADAMS. With a Frontispiece by GORDON BROWNE. *Crown 8vo.* 3*s.* 6*d.*

Leaders of Religion

Edited by H. C. BEECHING, M.A. *With Portrait, crown 8vo.* 2s. 6d.

A series of short biographies of the most prominent leaders of religious life and thought.

The following are ready—

2/6

CARDINAL NEWMAN. By R. H. HUTTON.

'Few who read this book will fail to be struck by the wonderful insight it displays into the nature of the Cardinal's genius and the spirit of his life.'—WILFRID WARD, in the *Tablet.*

'Full of knowledge, excellent in method, and intelligent in criticism. We regard it as wholly admirable.'—*Academy.*

JOHN WESLEY. By J. H. OVERTON, M.A.

'It is well done : the story is clearly told, proportion is duly observed, and there is no lack either of discrimination or of sympathy.'—*Manchester Guardian.*

BISHOP WILBERFORCE. By G. W. DANIEL, M.A.

CHARLES SIMEON. By H. C. G. MOULE, M.A.

Other volumes will be announced in due course.

University Extension Series

A series of books on historical, literary, and scientific subjects, suitable for extension students and home reading circles. Each volume is complete in itself, and the subjects are treated by competent writers in a broad and philosophic spirit.

Edited by J. E. SYMES, M.A.,

Principal of University College, Nottingham.

Crown 8vo. Price (with some exceptions) 2s. 6d.

The following volumes are ready :—

THE INDUSTRIAL HISTORY OF ENGLAND. By H. DE B. GIBBINS, M.A., late Scholar of Wadham College, Oxon., Cobden Prizeman. *Third Edition.* With Maps and Plans. 3s.

A compact and clear story of our industrial development. A study of this concise but luminous book cannot fail to give the reader a clear insight into the principal phenomena of our industrial history. The editor and publishers are to be congratulated on this first volume of their venture, and we shall look with expectant interest for the succeeding volumes of the series.'—*University Extension Journal.*

A HISTORY OF ENGLISH POLITICAL ECONOMY. By
L. L. PRICE, M.A., Fellow of Oriel College, Oxon.

PROBLEMS OF POVERTY: An Inquiry into the Industrial
Conditions of the Poor. By J. A. HOBSON, M.A.

VICTORIAN POETS. By A. SHARP.

THE FRENCH REVOLUTION. By J. E. SYMES, M.A.

PSYCHOLOGY. By F. S. GRANGER, M.A., Lecturer in Philosophy at University College, Nottingham.

THE EVOLUTION OF PLANT LIFE: Lower Forms. By
G. MASSEE, Kew Gardens. With Illustrations.

AIR AND WATER. Professor V. B. LEWES, M.A. Illustrated.

THE CHEMISTRY OF LIFE AND HEALTH. By C. W.
KIMMINS, M.A. Camb. Illustrated.

THE MECHANICS OF DAILY LIFE. By V. P. SELLS, M.A.
Illustrated.

ENGLISH SOCIAL REFORMERS. H. DE B. GIBBINS, M.A.

ENGLISH TRADE AND FINANCE IN THE SEVEN-
TEENTH CENTURY. By W. A. S. HEWINS, B.A.

Social Questions of To-day

Edited by H. DE B. GIBBINS, M.A.

Crown 8vo.   2s. 6d.

2/6

A series of volumes upon those topics of social, economic,
and industrial interest that are at the present moment fore-
most in the public mind. Each volume of the series is written by an
author who is an acknowledged authority upon the subject with which
he deals.

The following Volumes of the Series are ready :—

TRADE UNIONISM—NEW AND OLD. By G. HOWELL,
M.P., Author of 'The Conflicts of Capital and Labour.'

THE CO-OPERATIVE MOVEMENT TO-DAY. By G. J.
HOLYOAKE, Author of 'The History of Co-operation.'

MUTUAL THRIFT.   By Rev. J. FROME WILKINSON, M.A., Author of ' The Friendly Society Movement.'

PROBLEMS OF POVERTY : An Inquiry into the Industrial Conditions of the Poor.   By J. A. HOBSON, M.A.

THE COMMERCE OF NATIONS.   By C. F. BASTABLE, M.A., Professor of Economics at Trinity College, Dublin.

THE ALIEN INVASION. By W. H. WILKINS, B.A., Secretary to the Society for Preventing the Immigration of Destitute Aliens.

THE RURAL EXODUS.   By P. ANDERSON GRAHAM.

LAND NATIONALIZATION.   By HAROLD COX, B.A.

A SHORTER WORKING DAY.   By H. DE B. GIBBINS and R. A. HADFIELD, of the Hecla Works, Sheffield.

BACK TO THE LAND : An Inquiry into the Cure for Rural Depopulation.   By H. E. MOORE.

Edinburgh : T. & A. Constable, *Printers to Her Majesty.*

www.ingramcontent.com/pod-product-compliance
Lightning Source LLC
Chambersburg PA
CBHW030131030726
47498CB00007B/2645